DARKLY BEINGS

Claudia Lefeve

Sugar Skull Books

Sugar Skull Books

Cover art design by Karri Klawiter

ISBN: 0615876978
ISBN-13: 978-0615876979

Other books by Claudia Lefeve

Travelers Series
Parallel
Paradox
Paradigm

For my favorite Spanish teacher and mom,
Irene Gomez Ybarra.

One

The bell chimed as I wandered into the aging storefront.

Its decrepit state wasn't even the worse part; it was smack dab in the worst part of town. In fact, it was located in one of those seedy neighborhoods one had to be brave enough to venture into, even during the day. But this was exactly the type of place I knew I'd find what I was looking for. My afternoon foray to the bad part of town was for a remotely interesting project I had to complete for class.

An elderly black woman stepped out from behind the dark curtain and walked up to the counter upon hearing the bell. She had the kind of ageless appearance older black women seem to have that could keep you guessing as to their true age—timeless. Walking around the shop, I felt the woman's watchful eye behind me as I walked along the tables, as I inspected the odds and ends she had for sale in her little shop.

Satisfied I wasn't there to cause trouble or shoplift, the old woman finally spoke from behind the counter: "What you seek you will find at home."

She said it like some kind of fortuneteller in a fading carney. I just kept browsing her inventory, pretending I didn't hear her.

"The person you seek is at home," she repeated again, loud enough that I couldn't continue to ignore her. Only this time I caught the slightest hint of another accent hidden just below the surface of her thick New Orleans drawl. Haitian perhaps?

I stopped fiddling with the little dolls with the threaded crossed out eyes and looked at the old voodoo woman curiously. She had to be none other than Big Momma Ledoux, whose name was embossed in cracked red paint on the shingle dangling over the front door of the shop. "Is that so? How do you know I'm looking for someone?" I finally asked.

She grinned, exposing a perfectly bright pearly white smile against her dark espresso skin. The heft of her body caused her to waddle slightly as she walked closer to the counter. "Aren't we all looking for something, *cher*?"

And that's exactly why I didn't believe in all that magic, mumbo jumbo crap. People like Big Momma always stuck to the obvious to make you believe what they were saying was true. Sure, weren't we all looking for someone or something at one point or another? It was all just a big charade if you ask me. Magic, potions, and fortunes were all just a smokescreen to con gullible people out of their hard-earned money. You believed in it because you wanted to believe, not because it was truth.

The only reason I was in the voodoo shop in a back alley of New Orleans in the first place with was to do some last minute research for my final paper, entitled *"The Rise in Commercialism of Voodoo in Post-Katrina New Orleans."* And what better way to debunk all this hoodoo voodoo than to do some research for my paper and expose it for the sham it really was. Don't get me wrong, I had a varied interest in the cultures of the world, but I had reservations about some of the practices involving religion or folklore. I certainly wasn't in the market to buy any potions to find a lost love or to become rich overnight, and I sure as hell wasn't planning on taking the advice from the old lady who claimed to be a grand voodoo priestess, no matter what the placard out front said.

"My roommate is at work, so he's technically not lost," I said, with just a subtle hint of sarcasm, hoping she'd lose interest in me. But I knew that wasn't what she meant—not that there was any real meaning behind her words—but I wasn't going to tell her anything revealing about myself so she could use it against me later. That's how these fortune tellers and mystics worked, you see.

They get you to open up with personal information so they could regurgitate it later and claim they have actual insight into your future.

The woman kept on smiling. "*Cher*, you know that not the truth. That not be the person you seek. Go home," she instructed. "Go." She flapped her hands as if she were shooing a fly. "Your destiny awaits you."

And there it was again. That one little word that could turn a skeptic into a believer: truth.

Only this guy ain't buying.

☾

"Are you still with us, Mr. McKenna?"

Professor Burns loomed over my desk; the dark cast of his shadow slid over the table as my classmates snickered around me. It was obvious I'd been daydreaming. And while the dream I was all too familiar, having already invaded my sleep these past couple of nights, it was the first time they had ever invaded during the day. Ever since I visited that damned voodoo shop a week earlier, I couldn't get the old voodoo woman's words out of my head. She occupied my dreams at night and now my consciousness during the day. Unknown whispers seemed to nudge me to heed her advice. *Go home, cher*, she whispered, her lullaby lulling me to sleep.

"Wyatt McKenna," my professor repeated, pronouncing each syllable slowly, obviously annoyed at my lack of undivided attention.

"Huh? What?" I looked up to face my anthropology professor, who was waiting for me to reach for the final exam he flapped in front of me. I had spent half of the semester trying to keep a low profile in his class, so I was surprised he even remembered my name.

Better get this over with, I thought to myself as I snatched the exam from his outstretched hand. This was my last final before the end of the school term and marked my last year at Tulane. With my medical school acceptance letter sitting on my dresser at home, I knew I would never need anything like anthropology in the real word (I was going to be a doctor!). This class was officially classified as a freshman level elective, but I had procrastinated long enough. The sooner I finished this exam, the faster I could pack and go home for the summer.

Home.

To Caldero.

It was the place I had spent years searching for ways to escape, but couldn't wait to get back to once I was gone —even though I never did. Although for the life of me, I couldn't figure out why I had a sudden yearning to return. Why now? But ever since I visited Big Momma Ledoux, I had a longing to go home, even though there really wasn't anything keeping me bound to my hometown. Nothing, or no one, except for maybe Carmen. I smiled at the thought of her welcoming me home with open arms and a hug that only a person who raised you could give.

Now, the town of Caldero wasn't a bursting metropolis like Houston or Dallas. While most Texans tend to have a grandiose illusion when it comes to their home state, most cities and towns are actually quite small in contrast to their grandiose sense of self-worth. With only a few thousand residents, Caldero was home to the childhood I left behind, hidden smack-dab in the costal southern region of Texas, nestled along the Guadalupe River. If you blinked while driving down US 77, you'd surely miss it.

But the urge to return to the town of my birth was so strong, I could feel its pull in the pit of my stomach. By the time I had made my decision to go home over summer break, the tightness in my gut began to ease and I knew I had made the right choice. The only way I was ever going to feel any sort of peace, and perhaps even some closure, was to go back to Caldero.

My roommate Paul thought I was nuts. He was a first year resident at Tulane Medical Center and I hardly ever saw him due to the long hours he put in at the hospital. It was a mutual arrangement we'd both grown to respect—basically we kept out of each other's way—he was a busy doctor and I was studying like mad to become one.

"Dude, in the two years we've roomed together you've never mentioned anything about your hometown. Why do you suddenly feel the need to go to a place you never want to talk about?"

"It's just something I have to do," I said.

He wasn't entirely convinced. "It can't be that great of a place if you haven't missed it until now."

"Oh, I miss it alright. Especially the food." That was the truth. Lord knows you couldn't find decent Tex-Mex anywhere outside of Texas—especially if you grew up near the border where beans and tortillas were a staple at every meal.

"Just like that, huh? You're not even going to go through commencement?"

"Nope." It was two days after my last final and walking with my class at graduation wasn't an option I'd even considered. Graduation ceremonies were events best spent with families to celebrate your accomplishments and to offer proof that their hard money and sacrifice was worth that college diploma. I had no such person to share those precious Hallmark moments with. My mother hadn't even attended my high school graduation. Since I was sticking around Tulane for medical school, I always had that to look forward to.

Paul merely shook his head in confusion as I continued to pack my bags for the summer. It didn't take long before I finally settled into my vintage 1976 Ford pick-up (a hand-me-down from my late grandfather) and hauled me and my bags the five-hundred plus miles from New Orleans to Caldero. The stretch of highway faded in the reflection of the rearview mirror as I temporarily said good-bye to my new life and said hello again to my past one.

As I drove, singing along to Willie, Waylon, and Johnny, the memories of my childhood surfaced, and for the most part they were pleasant ones. Well, as good as they could be, considering the circumstances that ultimately drove me away.

I continued to reminisce about my childhood on the drive down until I reached the uneven road that marked the entrance to our driveway. The demons I fought so hard to run from greeted me as soon as the tires hit the caliche drive toward the house. Some memories were meant to be buried. It was that reason alone I dreaded coming home, the reason I had refused for the last four years to come home during holiday and summer breaks. But the pull to return to Caldero was strong.

Two

Most of the homes in my neighborhood were constructed back in the early 1840's, upon the heels of antebellum Texas—before the war for state independence, not the Civil War—built by the original Irish *empresarios* who settled before the period of statehood when the land was still Mexican soil. To even call it a neighborhood was stretching it. Most of the surrounding homes were built on several acres of land, allowing enough privacy to ensure the neighbors weren't snooping out their windows (though that didn't keep the rumor mill from shutting down). And even though I was a McKenna and could trace my ancestors all the way back to the town's humble beginnings, this apple didn't exactly fall from the wealthy branch of the family tree. We only lived in the grand house

I called my childhood home because my mother had inherited it lock, stock, and barrel from one of her great aunts. Which was a good thing, all things considered.

My body sat rigid in the bench seat of my beat-up old Ford, staring at the stately aging Greek Revival that awaited my return. If I didn't know any better, I'd say the house was staring right back at me. Carmen must have had candles burning in the house, for the flames cast an ominous flicker against the glass, as if the house had eyes that gleamed with delight to see her prodigal son return.

The memories I thought I'd left behind weren't always bad ones. For a long time, they were actually good, or at least, the fond memories of that of a ten year-old boy. That was before my father decided to leave me and mom, and before my mom took to drinking.

I managed to scramble out of the truck's cab, and I loitered on the front porch just a moment longer than necessary before I had the courage to enter the house. Then again, I didn't have to enter through the front entryway; my bedroom had its own entrance from the outside (the old servants' quarters) with a set of stairs that ran up the side of the house directly to my room. I could have avoided a welcome home scene all together, which believe me was tempting, but I was curious to see if she would be there to greet me.

With an ounce of courage, I finally entered the aging house but stood fixed in the foyer, not knowing if my mother remembered I was coming home. I wasn't betting any money on it. She had her good days and bad days and what I was willing to bet on was her fading memory. For awhile, well before I went away to school, she had more lucid days than not, but as the years went on, those days were few and far between. My own memory was lapsing as I couldn't even remember whether or not I had called ahead for her to expect me.

But there was someone who did remember, so perhaps I did call ahead after all.

"Wyatt! You home!" Carmen said in her broken English, forever forgetting her linking verbs and adjectives, despite living most of her adult life here in Texas. Most of her English was picked up around the house and from watching daytime soap operas (in the evenings it was *telenovelas*).

María Carmen Esparza Portillo was everything my mother wasn't: loving, maternal, and most importantly, available. She had come to work for our family when my mother was a little girl and had stayed on to take care of me after I was born. It wasn't uncommon to have live-in help around these parts; that was just the way it done the closer you were to the border: Mexican immigrants seeking work in the States, with women leaving their homes at a young age only to be employed as nannies and housekeepers in order to send money back home. But after awhile, they became members of the family they worked for—which was the case with Carmen.

Barely standing five feet tall and finally beginning to show her true age, Carmen was still a force to be reckoned with. As strict as a Catholic school nun, she made sure I had a proper upbringing, manners and all. Her greying hair, fashioned in her trademark bun at the base of her neck, and her faded flowered house dress were truly a sight for sore eyes. I had to admit, I was more grateful for Carmen's homecoming welcome than if it had come from my own mother.

"I made your favorite," she said, her 'y's' sounding more like 'j's'. "*Andale*, we go to the kitchen."

"Where's Mom?" I didn't have to ask, but I did out of some sense of obligation. I knew she was holed up in her room, either too drunk to make it down the stairs or completely passed out. My mother's spiral into alcoholism had gotten worse over the years, and I was sure it hadn't improved in all the time I'd been gone. In the beginning, it was just a couple of cocktails before dinner, but it gradually progressed to drinking as soon as she was awake enough to pour and getting plastered before noon.

Her dark brown eyes glanced upwards. "She upstairs, napping," she said, confirming my suspicions. As an afterthought she added, "*Mijito*, you know she care about you," noting the disappointment in my eyes.

That was her pet name for me, which was a form of slang, combing the words *mi* and *hijo*— *mijo* or 'my son.' It was considered a term of endearment around these parts and it wasn't limited to just family members. To hear her say it now reminded me there were others who actually cared whether or not I was around, even if my own mother couldn't be bothered.

"I know, I just thought she'd make an effort. I haven't been home in four years," I pointed out, hoping she'd understand my side.

"You should come home sooner. You make your mom very upset," she chastised instead, oblivious to how I felt on the matter.

Despite her scolding, I grinned because I couldn't help myself. It was just like old times. If I wasn't careful, Carmen would send me up to my room without dinner. She had a knack for making you feel like a small child, even as an adult, when you did something disrespectful.

Somehow, I doubted my mom even noticed my absence, but I wasn't going to voice my opinion. "I had a lot going on with school and work, Carmen. You know I would have come down if I had the chance." It was a lie and we both knew it, but Carmen didn't contradict or reprimand me this time. As much as she liked to defend her, she also knew how hurt I was by mother's absence and forgave me the little white lie.

Instead, she simply clicked her tongue in disapproval and said, "It's no nice, no coming home."

"I'm sorry Carmen. I'm home now." But I knew simple words alone wouldn't be enough to appease Carmen. "For the whole summer and I promise I'll come down more often," I added. It was a lie and I knew it. Once I started med school, I'd be even more absent from the life I once knew.

I gave her a peck on the cheek as she slid a plate of steaming tamales in front of me. Tamales were normally reserved for Christmastime, as preparing them was labor intensive, but she knew pork tamales were my favorite. Grateful for the special treat, I didn't say a word, in fear she'd then scold me for not coming home during the holidays.

After scarfing down the entire plate of tamales, I informed Carmen of my plans to meet up with the gang later that night at the river. I hadn't even been home an hour and I was already planning to take my leave again. Then again, it wasn't like my mother was around to notice anyway. Another point I didn't bring up again in front of Carmen.

She nodded, not entirely surprised by my announcement of my evening plans. "Before you go out with friends, go to the De Leóns. I run low on herbs and tobacco," she said.

Aside from working for our family, Carmen was also a faith healer. *Curanderas* as they were called around these parts, and when she thought my mother and I weren't paying attention—which wasn't too hard considering my mother's current state—she could be found on the back of the wrap-around porch reading people's fate, doing cleansings, and mixing love potions for the lovelorn. It wasn't until I was in junior high that I caught on to Carmen's moonlighting gig. Up until then, I just thought she had a lot of friends and enjoyed entertaining out on the back porch.

I didn't know if any of that faith healing stuff actually worked—it couldn't possibly, but by the stream of visitors Carmen had, she must have been doing something right. When she wasn't courting clients, or performing a cleansing, she'd spend most of her time praying and lighting religious candles around the house. Her favorite was St. Jude, the patron saint of lost causes—I'm sure she figured my mother and I could use all the help we could get.

Despite what one might think about small southern towns, the practice of *curanderismo* was alive and well the closer you got to the Mexican border, and it wasn't necessarily kept a secret or considered taboo in a town like Caldero. If you were ever in the market for spiritual guidance, all you had to do was drive around some of the lower income neighborhoods and if you saw a line forming at the door, the homeowner was either selling tortillas by the dozen or dispensing charms to ward off hexes. And in Carmen's case, selling her herbs and peace of mind. It wasn't so different from Louisiana, I realized, except instead of practicing *curanderismo* it was *voodoo*.

As contradictory as it may appear, the irony over my skepticism over anything involving magic and being brought up by a Mexican faith healer wasn't lost on me. The way I saw it, Carmen and her clientele could believe anything they wanted. But that didn't mean I had to buy a ticket to the show.

The last thing I wanted to do was go by the De Leóns to pick up healing supplies. It wasn't that I disliked the sisters—I liked them very much, in fact—but I had plans to meet everyone down on the Guadalupe. Even though I'd been gone a good while, I was pleased to find that it was still tradition to meet at the river once everyone returned home for the summer. I'd already been in touch with my best friend Tyler to solidify the plans for the evening. He was in charge of bringing the keg and all I had to do was show up. But there was really no point in denying Carmen; she'd only end up winning, so I just nodded in agreement.

Three

The De León sisters owned a small restaurant right in the center of town, El Pozo Hondo, meaning deep well, otherwise known as The Pit—mostly in reference to the large earthen pit in the back used for *barbacoa*, but in actuality the moniker was just easier for us *gringos* to say. But like true entrepreneurs, it wasn't the only business they ran. Like Carmen, these women were also faith healers—if I believed in such things, of course. And even though I didn't, something made me suspect that if magic were real, the De León sisters were legit. Customers left their restaurant with either their bellies full or their souls restored—sometimes a little bit of both.

In their own right, the sisters were considered a living landmark in the history of Caldero. While they were both born in Texas, the sisters remained a step half-way between the new world and the old world. Second generation Texans, Ester De León was the eldest of the two and was stuck somewhere between Texas and Mexico, forever speaking Spanglish. Her younger sister Amelia was the polar opposite, embracing her Texas roots, boasting big Texas hair—"the higher the hair, the closer to God," she was always fond of saying—and the one responsible for the best chicken fried steak this side of the Guadalupe, or the Guada-LOOP, as the locals liked to pronounce it. There wasn't a Texan good ol' boy within a one hundred mile radius that would contest it, it was that good.

Their eclectic differences was also reflected in their choice restaurant decor. Knick-knacks from Mexico coupled with tacky Texas souvenirs decorated the place. Everything from political commentaries (an "I Miss Reagan" bumper sticker was stuck under a fading poster of Poncho Villa), to their celebrity hall of fame photos strategically placed on the far side of the wall near the kitchen— boasting snapshots of the two grinning sisters with the likes of Chuck Norris, Mary Kay Ash (of Mary Kay Cosmetics), and Claudia "Lady Bird" Johnson (the sisters maintain to this day that the former First Lady came for a personal visit back in 1964, but in truth, Mrs. Johnson's car had broken down on her way to a political campaign rally and she had needed to use their phone).

After dinner, I debated whether or not to check in on my mother and decided against it, opting to head straight to The Pit before meeting up with the others at the river. Knowing the sisters, I knew they'd want to chit-chat, so I wanted to get a head start.

For the first time since setting foot in Caldero, as soon as I stepped into the restaurant, I knew I was home. The smell of enchiladas, coupled with the sweet aroma of fresh *pan dulce* displayed prominently in the pastry case, warmed me in the same way a grandson visiting his grandma's would. There was a name for that feeling: nostalgia. It was as if time stood still and I never left. Nothing had changed in the four years I'd been gone.

In true Texas fashion, it didn't take but a second of walking in the place for the pleasantries to commence. "And to what do we owe the pleasure of your company, Wyatt?" Amelia De León greeted me, ruffling my hair. "You need a haircut," she added, eying my somewhat overgrown sandy blonde shag.

I smoothed my hair back and grinned. "Your food, of course. Hard to find good eats like yours in New Orleans," I said. Not that there's anything wrong with Louisiana cuisine, but Tex-Mex was considered haute cuisine. Louisiana may have cornered the market on beignets, gumbo, and oyster po' boys, but here in the southern part of Texas, it was all about beer, beans, barbeque, and anything you can wrap inside a warm tortilla.

Amelia beamed at the praise. "Aren't you a dear child?"

I smiled once again at the fading Texan belle with her big-beehive-bar hair. The De Leóns might be a little weird at times, but their motherly fuss made you dismiss half their quirkiness. I had momentarily succumbed enticing aroma from the kitchen and almost forgotten what had brought me to their restaurant in the first place. "Oh, and Carmen wanted me to come by and ask if you had any herbs and tobacco," I whispered, lest any of the customers overhead me.

She nodded, noting my embarrassment over the subject matter. "Of course. Now, you just find yourself a booth and I'll get that ready for you."

I turned toward the row of booths by the front windows. That's when I noticed her sitting there, her nose buried in what looked like a book, or possibly even the menu; the top of the booth obscuring the table. I almost tripped making my way near her table.

At first glance, there was nothing extraordinary about her, but she made me almost stop in my tracks just the same. For one thing, I knew pretty much everyone in town. That was the way around here—you knew everyone, and their cousin's cousin, and their sister's cousin's cousin. And she was most definitely not a cousin. She was a new face in Caldero. And secondly, I could tell she was more than just a "somebody or other" sitting all alone in a booth in the middle of nowhere.

The rush I felt upon seeing her there in that booth came to me in that instant—like a dream you suddenly recall weeks later, like a sudden wave of déjà vu, or when you have a thought dangling in the back of your mind that finally ripples off the tongue when you least expect it. That is what it felt like to lay eyes upon her for the first time.

After what seemed like being momentarily stuck on pause, I finally found my balance and made my way over to where she was sitting. She looked quite content to sit alone, but I couldn't help myself. I was never one for being shy and I saw no reason why I couldn't introduce myself. As I got closer, I realized she wasn't reading a book, but was studying a line of cards in front of her.

"Are those tarot cards?" They certainly looked like tarot cards, only different—girly almost. They weren't anything like the kind Carmen used when she did her readings. Once, when I was sixteen, she'd caught me snooping in her room where I'd discovered her tarot deck. But instead of old-fashioned, creepy-looking cards like the ones Carmen had, this set featured cute, cartoonish female characters. I watched as she kept flipping the cards and almost did a double take. I swear there was one image that looked very much like the character Samantha Stephens from *Bewitched*. Another one looked suspiciously like Vanna White. Then again, I could have been mistaken.

"Yup," she said, never looking up from her cards.

"What are they telling you?" Even though Carmen never made her card reading a secret, I never had the nerve to talk to her about it. The day I discovered the cards hidden in her room, she scolded me something fierce and I never ventured uninvited into her room again. I don't know if it was the wrath of Carmen herself or the hideous cards, but either way, I never inquired about it again. It always seemed that it was a private matter between she and her clients. In all honesty, I never really gave it much thought after that day in Carmen's room. Until now.

This time, the girl did look up and when she did, I noticed she had the most brilliant blue eyes I'd ever seen. I stopped myself before I stared into them too long and embarrassed us both. It was certainly not a sight I expected. It was almost as if her eyes were an afterthought; a striking contrast against her tanned skin and dark hair.

There was something else about her that struck me as odd: she didn't necessarily strike me as a mystic kind of girl who read tarot cards. Not that there's a specific type or anything, but around here, unless you're an old lady that practices the ways of the old world, like Carmen or the De León sisters, reading cards was reserved for the wannabe goth-type girls. There were a couple of those back in high school, and even at college, but this girl didn't seem to fit the bill. She was dressed simply in cut-off jeans that looked to be a tad on the short side and a plain white t-shirt. Nothing striking or unusual about her appearance—aside from those glorious eyes—except that her feet were bare, her flip-flops discarded beneath the table. Her bright red pedicured feet stuck out from beneath the table, resting on other side of the booth's bench (her legs were that long). Not that she'd uttered so much as a word other than "yup," but she also gave off the impression that she was smart. Not just brainy book smart, but intelligent—bare feet and all.

Now that I had the opportunity to see her up close, there was no question she wasn't from around here. If I had to venture a guess, I'd figure she was in her early twenties, so we would certainly have crossed paths in school. And if I had gone to school with her, I would have definitely remembered. Still, she had to come from somewhere. "So, you new in town?"

Again, no response. She tilted her head to the side as if to question me and my intentions. I hadn't exactly offered her a pick-up line, but it was as if she didn't hear me or simply didn't want to. I decided to try a different approach. "Do you have a name?"

"It's Natalia," one of the De León sisters answered for her, coming out from the kitchen with two brown paper bags in hand. "Our niece is staying with us this summer."

"I prefer Natalie," she finally said, looking cross at her aunt, annoyed by the intrusion, as if her aunt had said the unthinkable. "Natalie Betancourt."

"Natalia, Natalie, what's the difference?" Amelia asked.

"The difference is, it's a lot easier to say Natalie."

"This is Texas. Everyone speaks Spanish. I bet even Wyatt knows a little," she said, tilting her head in my direction.

It was true. Raised primarily by Carmen, I'd picked up some here and there. Even though Carmen spoke English the majority of the time, she still mumbled and cursed in her native language when she thought no one was paying attention. When I was younger, she even allowed me to stay up late to watch *telenovelas* with her.

"Whatever, I like Natalie better. Can we just leave it at that?" It was clear she wanted the two of us to disappear so she could go back to reading her tarot cards.

Her aunt just pursed her lips before turning her attention back at me. "Wyatt, I wrapped up the herbs for Carmen and added a few extra spices," she said, lifting up a smaller second package.

Natalie shot me a look, probably wondering why her aunt was giving me a sack of healing herbs. This seemed to elicit the attention I had wished for earlier when I initially approached her. I'm sure she was curious as to why I would need faith healing remedies since I was pretty sure she knew about her aunts' side business.

Amelia quickly changed the subject. "I have a great idea. Why don't you let Wyatt show you around town sometime? You could use a few friends to hang out with besides moping around the restaurant," she suggested.

"*Tía*, I already told you, I'm fine. I don't need a tour guide."

"Suit yourself, but you'll be here awhile. It might help if you made some friends." She cupped Natalie's chin with her hand. "It can get very lonely here."

From the look that passed between each other, there was something I was obviously missing, as if this had been a point of contention between them for awhile. What did Natalie have against making new friends? I was certainly open to the possibility if it meant spending more time with her.

Amelia shrugged her shoulders as if to say, "I tried."

After her flat-out refusal to have me show her around town, I decided it was worth a shot to invite her out again anyway. "Some of us are meeting up tonight at the river. Since you're new and all, maybe you'd like to come?"

"No thanks."

"You sure? The river's a lot of fun. There's a keg and everything. A few of the girls will be there too." I added the last part in just in case she had reservations about going to a party with a total stranger. Plus, I didn't want her thinking it was just me and a bunch of guys.

She looked up for the second time with those wide blue eyes that were still beautiful even when she looked annoyed. "Even worse. I'll pass, but thanks for the offer." She ran her hand over the cards and scooped them up in her hands one swoop, like a seasoned Vegas dealer, and put them back into their purple tin container.

"Suit yourself." I couldn't force her to go and it was probably for the best. She didn't exactly seem like the kind of girl that would have a good time at a kegger by the river. I couldn't say I blamed her. Now that I was older, it wasn't exactly my idea of a good time either, but around here, it was easy to fall back into old routines.

Four

Aside from my estranged home life situation, there were some advantages to coming home—like reclaiming my former football-star status. I know it sounds conceited to feel that way, but when I first arrived at Tulane, I was a nobody, just an incoming fish in an oversized fish bowl, swimming furiously in order to survive my first year. Four years later, I wasn't any more popular, but then again, it was New Orleans after all—it was more like a big tank. But here, I was still good ol' Wyatt McKenna, former star quarterback with a district championship title under his belt. So in a way, it felt good to be back.

Kelsey Powers must have thought so, too. It didn't take her long to notice my beater truck pulling up next to the other gleaming, newer pick-up models and was poised to greet me as I stepped out of the truck's cab.

Kelsey—the girl I'd left behind.

Seemed like I left a lot of things back here in Caldero. Some things obviously more pleasant than others. The lithe, blond petite was certainly a sight for sore eyes, but that's about all it was—just a sight. A glimpse into my past and why I tried so hard to run away from it.

Back then, Kelsey was the captain of the cheerleading team to my quarterback status on the football team. From the outside looking in, we were the power couple. The couple everyone wanted to be, the couple everyone aspired to be, and the couple everyone envied. As I look back at our relationship, I realized how superficial it all actually was. But none of that mattered in high school and I had to admit, it wasn't all bad, being with a girl like Kelsey. She was beautiful, popular, and most importantly (to a teenager with raging hormones), easy. Being able to sleep with a girl like her at any given time was every horny teenage boy's wet dream. No, sir, not a bad deal at all.

"Wyatt, you're back! How's New Orleans? You know, I missed you," she said pouting, biting her bottom lip in a way only beautiful girls like her could pull off. I knew she didn't really give two shits one way or another, given our mutual break-up years ago, but it did serve as a small reminder that I had been absent for too long, making me feel ashamed for the second time that day, but the moment lasted only but a second. Leave it to Kelsey to bring up a sore subject.

"Sorry, Kels, I just had a lot going on with school and just never had the chance 'til now." While technically everything I said was true, I didn't just have the guts to tell her the real reason I hadn't come home. Seeing my mother in such a degenerative state before I left for Tulane, I decided I needed more time before I had the strength to return. If Kelsey had been a better girlfriend back in high school, she would have easily understood my reluctance to come home after all these years.

For a brief moment, it was like I'd been transported back in time, except I was well aware I was only re-living the past, if only for a brief moment in time. High school sweethearts broken up by the prospects of better options, the expectations of college and new beginnings. It was the tragic standard cliché that could befall a young love. Even Kelsey knew on some level the artificial nature of our relationship. That was part of her repertoire: being artificial in every aspect of her life, from her highlighted bleached blonde hair to her fake acrylic nails. Even her relationships were phony on her end.

"I was beginning to think you'd up and forgotten all about me," she began to complain again.

"Never," I lied. After three damn years, did she really expect me to harbor feelings for her or even care?

She didn't fool me for a second. I knew she hadn't really given much thought about me either after she herself went away to school. My suspicions were that she didn't want to hang around town all summer alone and believed I was the one to ease that boredom for the next couple of months.

"Well, just so you know, I've been pretty busy myself," Kelsey said.

"Oh yeah?" Somehow, I found it highly doubtful she thought much of me at all. We went our separate ways after high school and never looked back, with me heading to New Orleans, while she had packed her bags to attend Texas State University in San Marcos.

Kelsey took me by the elbow and steered me toward the river where our friends awaited, as she spoke about the fabulous time she was having at school. "And you'll never guess who was elected chapter president of her sorority," she went on. She was talking about herself of course.

"Sounds great." It didn't actually, but I humored her just the same. Since we were both here, it seemed best to make the most of it, even it if meant rekindling old flames, if just for the summer. But thoughts of the long-legged girl at The Pit filtered through my mind as I took Kelsey's hand while we made our way down the river bank to join the others.

"Wyatt, over here!" The sound of my best friend shouting my name was like a cow bell beckoning you to dinner. Paul, my roommate back at Tulane, was fine and all, and I considered him as good a friend as any, but I missed my childhood friend. It was the kind of friendship you couldn't forge past the age of eight, in a time when being blood brothers was the first commitment you ever made with another person. And aside from a few emails here and there, I really hadn't stayed in touch with my best friend. It wasn't like they depicted it in the sappy TV commercials; guys just didn't do long distance phone calls. Any opportunity I'd had to see him was lost when I didn't come down for a visit all those Thanksgiving or Christmas breaks. Hell, I didn't even party with him down in South Padre during Spring Break. I was afraid that if I had, I would have been obligated to make a detour to Caldero.

"Ty!" I slapped him on the back, which is the male equivalent of a hug. "When did you get back in town?" Tyler had landed a football scholarship to Texas A&M and in four years had made quite a name for himself. Rumor had it, he might even be drafted for the NFL. Occasionally, when I wasn't studying or working part-time, I was able to catch a couple of college games on television. He was every bit the football star that I myself had been back in high school. Only he was the true talent and I was small potatoes—I hadn't even been sought by the scouts.

"Hey, Ty. You're lookin' good," Kelsey chimed in.

Tyler never shied away from a compliment, even if it came from Kelsey. "What's up yourself, good looking?"

Even though he was my best friend and she my ex-girlfriend, it still didn't stop him from hitting on her. It really was like old times. Tyler was considered the Lothario of Caldero and you could never take him seriously when it came to women. Or was it, he never took women seriously? Either way, he'd been my blood brother since we were five and I never judged him or his sexual escapades.

"Hey, speaking of, how easy are the girls over in The Big Easy?" Tyler asked, laughing at his own pun.

"I wouldn't know. Spent most of my time studying and working."

"That's right. Wyatt here is going to be a rich doctor one day," Kelsey said, eyes twinkling at the prospect. My suspicions about her intentions were confirmed. She was trying to get into my good graces again, but we were a thing of the past. The one I fought so hard to leave behind. There was no way I was going to allow myself to end up like most of the men in this town: married to their high school sweetheart, stuck with an aging beauty queen (knowing her mother, Kelsey wasn't going to age gracefully), forever trapped here in town with no options.

"Uh, not quite," I said.

A small wrinkle formed on Kelsey's otherwise unblemished forehead. She didn't like to be corrected, especially in front of others. "How's that?"

"For starters, I haven't even started med school yet. And most doctors generally don't bring in the big bucks until later in their career," I said.

She rolled her eyes in annoyance. "What are you trying to say?"

God, was she always this dense back in high school? Yeah, she probably was, only I was too concerned with getting into her pants to notice. "Well, student loans will be— " I started to explain.

Tyler placed his arm over my shoulders, leading me in the direction the bonfire that already had folks gathered around it. "That's enough lecture talk for one evening. The beer's right over there and it's getting warm, so come on," Tyler said.

It was almost like an unofficial class reunion— everyone was down on the Guada-LOOP tonight. Even those who'd graduated well before I had come out for the occasion. Which only proves that if you stick around here long past graduation, your social options are greatly reduced. There's not much to do around here than to gather around, drink beer, and talk about the good ol' days.

Perhaps all the reminiscing ended up not being such a good thing after all. After one too many beers, I ended up away from the others, alone with Kelsey, further down the river's path, near the far edge of the river bank. Even though the live oak trees filtered the moonlit night, I could tell she was still that beautiful girl from high school, but being alone with her was not what I had in mind when I left the house earlier that evening. She just didn't hold my attention like she used to. So what was I doing here with her now?

We were lying on our backs, looking up at the stars that shone through the tree limbs above, when she ran her hand under my shirt—the cold chill of her hands on my chest giving me goose-bumps. "We used to be good," she murmured.

"Huh?" Clearly I had no idea what she was talking about, but yet, at the same time, I did. I just wanted to ignore it.

She started to unbutton my shirt. "You, the captain of the football team, me the head cheerleader. We could be like that again."

"That was years ago," I pointed out. But Kelsey wasn't exactly off-base. We *were* pretty good—physically good—but when you're young and stupid, everything seemed like a good time. Now that I've had a chance to grow up, distance myself from the fold, I knew there was more to life than just perky cheerleaders and a quick romp in the back of my pick-up truck. I pushed away her hand that had made its way down my crotch. "Come on Kels. Think about what you're saying."

"I know exactly what I'm saying," she hiccuped. Which wasn't very attractive considering she was trying to seduce me. That's when Kelsey took the opportunity and kissed me. For a second, I tried to resist, but my reservations, no thanks to my inebriated state, soon gave in to temptation. Surprisingly, the familiarity of it all was comforting. It might be the only pleasant experience I would have while being home, so I embraced the moment. I just had to make sure not to let things go too far. I didn't want to have to deal with Kelsey following me around all summer thinking we were something more than just friends.

After a few minutes of heavy fondling, I could have sworn I heard a rustling behind the trees. I brushed off Kelsey's advances for a moment to see if it was Tyler or one of the other guys that had found us. I waited for the barrage of heckling—which we'd no doubt deserve—that never came. But no one was there. Or if there was, they left quickly. Maybe whoever it was saw us preoccupied, decided it wasn't any of their business, and went back to party with the others. There was no excuse for my behavior with Kelsey, but God help me, I couldn't help myself. It felt good to feel her touch—any woman's touch —it'd been so long. I'd buried myself in my studies these last few years and had forgotten what it was like to be physically close to someone.

It was well past midnight by the time Kelsey and I finally emerged from the wooded area and rejoined the rest of the gang. By then most had either gone home or were too drunk to go anywhere. It looked like a couple of guys had the good sense to bring along their tents; I spotted a few erected along the line of cars and trucks still parked. Since it'd been awhile since I downed my last beer and felt relatively sober, I decided to go on home and sleep off the past day's events. In hindsight, I should have done what some of the others had done and slept in my truck or even crashed in someone's tent. I hadn't even taken a moment to rest after driving back from Louisiana earlier in the day. Was it only just today I drove into town? I wanted to lie in a real bed—my bed—and I didn't want to take a chance that Kelsey was up for an encore performance. As much as I enjoyed our little foray by the river, it was a one-shot deal as far as I was concerned, so in the end, against my better judgment, I decided to drive home.

I should have been paying better attention to the road and not thinking about Natalie—the girl with the long legs and mesmerizing blue eyes. Just as I made the turnoff to my road, I glimpsed an unusually large bird heading straight in my direction. It was an owl. At first, I thought it was the moonlight playing tricks on my eyes, until I noticed the bird was twice as large as any owl I'd ever seen. I slowed the truck down to a crawl as I continued to stare at the owl flying low in the distance; it was headed straight toward my windshield. I continued to stare at the curious bird and couldn't help but feel that its eyes held something human.

I managed to swerve the truck away from the massive bird and narrowly avoided clipping the large oak tree on the side of the road. I slammed on the breaks and glanced at the rearview mirror to see if the large owl was still there or if it had taken off. Nothing. I even got out of the truck to make sure I hadn't hit it, even though I knew I hadn't, but there was nothing there. Perhaps it was my mind playing tricks on me after all.

Five

The events of the previous day took its toll on me the next morning. Not just the drive home, but the beer, the near miss with the owl, meeting Natalie, messing around with Kelsey—everything. It was a lot to process even after a somewhat decent night's sleep. Technically, I was on summer vacation, so I didn't have to wake up early, but I still felt somewhat guilty about sleeping in. As I made my way down to the kitchen, I wasn't the only one that took notice of the late morning hour.

"Your breakfast get cold, so I throw out," Carmen said, pointing to the trash can. "Next time, you be up before I cook."

I didn't have to peer into the trash to know she had made chorizo and eggs for breakfast. My stomach growled over the lingering scent of the spicy sausage and tortillas that still permeated the air in the kitchen.

My first full official day back and I'd already committed the first cardinal sin: Don't be late for breakfast. It was one thing to skip breakfast with advance notice, but it was quite another to show up late at the table after Carmen had already begun cooking. And thinking of skipping breakfast, I wondered whether my mother would come out of her room to make an appearance. It was too early to drink (even she had her standards), unless of course it was a Bloody Mary, a mimosa, or some other alcoholic beverage she deemed socially acceptable to consume during morning hours. "Sorry, Carmen. Has Mom come down yet?"

For all my protests about seeing my mother and my reluctance to come home to visit, deep down I wished my mother would make an effort to be a real mom. The scars I carried from her emotional abandonment long ago, were cut so deep I'd been in denial about my feelings. I loved my mother. I just wish she'd love me back.

She clicked her tongue in disapproval, either at me or my mother I wasn't sure. "She had longer night than you."

Carmen didn't have to elaborate further. Well before I moved away to school, when I was in grade school, my mother made it a point to go into what I liked to call a cocktail stupor at least once a week. She'd roam the house pulling out old photos of her and my father. It was a weekly ritual I grew to resent. For awhile, I thought she'd grow tired of torturing herself. Once, I even tried to hide the family photos from her usual hiding spots, hoping she'd forget. She had not only found them, but tore into me for trying to meddle during her healing process. That's what she actually said, her "healing process," as if the liquor could drown the demons that had invaded her soul —but it was obvious self-medicating wasn't getting the job done. By the time I was a junior in high school, she had turned her weekly stupors into a daily occurrence.

I'll never forget that last night with my mother before heading off to Tulane. It didn't take a shrink to figure out she had associated my leaving for college with my father's abandonment all those years ago. It didn't matter to her that it was a different situation entirely. I wasn't abandoning her like my dad had, but she considered it one and the same. The irony was, by her getting loaded every night and cutting me off emotionally, she was doing exactly what my father had done to us. If it hadn't been for Carmen, I would have been all alone.

I had my acceptance letter months before I finally told her. Part of me was a coward for waiting so long, but it was partly my mother's fault. She was never sober long enough to talk to. I found her in the living room when I finally broke the news to her. The room was unnaturally dark, with the curtains shut to prevent the fading afternoon sun from peeking through the windows. My mother claimed the sun gave her headaches, so we were all forced to go without natural or even superficial lighting in the house whenever she was around. I didn't have the heart to argue that it was the booze that caused the headaches, which in turn caused the sensitivity to light.

"Why do you have to go so far away?" she had cried, when I finally told her of my plans to go away to school.

"I already told you, Tulane was the only school to offer me a full ride," I said. My mom never worked a day in her life, so funds were rather limited. The only reason we managed to scrape by all these years after my father left—and managed to keep Carmen employed—was through a trust set up by my mother's family. It wasn't much, but it provided enough for us to be fed and pay for the essentials like utilities. From an early age, I knew the only way I could afford to go to school was through scholarships and limited financial aid. Only I lied. Tulane wasn't the only school that offered me money. Most of the major universities in Texas I applied to—A&M, UT, Baylor, Rice—also offered up nice financial packages, but no campus or curriculum was more appealing to me at the time than the one more than five hundred miles away.

"But it's in Louisiana!"

"You make it sound like I'm moving to another country. It's only a day's drive away, Mom."

She had stuck her hand in her robe pocket and pulled out a photo, presumably one of she and my father, as she took a swig of her drink in the other. By that point, she had taken to storing flasks or those little mini airplane bottles of liquor in the pockets of her clothing. "That's what you promised," she whispered in response. It wasn't directed at me but the faded photograph in her hand.

"Promises and obligations," she yelled up at the ceiling as she paced the floor. "Only they weren't promises. Not to me."

I couldn't bear to see my mother like this, but I didn't dare leave the room, not wanting to add fuel to her delusions that I was leaving her for good. But in the larger scheme of things, by going away to school, I was doing exactly that—feeding into that paranoia in which the men in her life would ultimately leave. I was worried about her psychological and physical well-being. Her self-medicating methods to cope with my father's abandonment only made her more anxious and unstable.

"Empty, empty," she sang, again to the ceiling. "But full of lies."

"Mom," I said, trying to calm her down. I'd seen her drunk a million times, but nothing like this. The vision of my mother in her satin negligee and skimpy silk robe only made her emphasized movements more grotesque. By then, my mother's health was already deteriorating—with alcohol and mixers being her main source of nutrition, her already small frame was reduced to mere skin and bones—although I suspect Carmen made her eat something when she could. My mother parading around in frilly nightgowns during all hours of the day only made her appear that much more macabre.

She stopped long enough to stare and ask me a direct question. For a second, she actually appeared sober and alert, much like her old self again. "Tell me, Wyatt, is the glass half full or empty?"

"Mom," I said, taking that small window of opportunity to reason with her, but I had a feeling that even though she was speaking directly to me, I don't think she was really talking me or anyone at all for that matter. Maybe she was speaking to the ghost of my father whose presence still lingered in the house like bad fish.

She suddenly grabbed my arms and shook me hard, the alcohol in her system making her stronger rather than weak. "Don't you see? It's already begun! Don't let them take you from me," she cried. "The two will become one and then you'll be lost."

Before I had a chance to ask her who they were or what she was talking about, Carmen stepped in without so much as a word to me and led my mother upstairs to her room. In a lot of ways, she was the worst enabler of all. Always coming to my mother's aid and defense.

That was the last time I saw my mother.

My mother must have already been down for the count by the time I got home. "Great, glad I missed it," I mumbled under my breath, low enough for Carmen not to hear. It should have bothered me that I had yet to see my mother since coming back to town, but didn't—at least, not on the surface. I'd become quite adept at keeping my emotions in check when it came to my mother.

If I were being honest with myself, what I really felt was fear. Fear that I would never be able to have a real relationship with my mother. Fear that she was broken to the point beyond repair that we would never be able to mend our differences. Fear that in a few years, maybe months, I would lose the last parent I had left.

Brushing those thoughts aside for a moment, content to let my subconscious deal with them as I always did, I left Carmen to do whatever it was she does around the house, and since I hadn't had breakfast yet—no thanks to me—I decided to head on over to The Pit. I also wouldn't mind seeing Natalie again, assuming she'd still be around. But Amelia had said her niece was staying for the entire summer.

Just like me.

Six

No such luck, I realized after I arrived at the restaurant. I had high hopes that the newest resident of Caldero would be in, eating breakfast or at least helping her aunts with the late breakfast rush. I still wasn't sure if she even worked at the restaurant, but it was still a good enough excuse to check it out. But at least I was one for two: the sisters were still serving breakfast. No one was around to take my order, so I pushed the swinging door that led into the kitchen. That was kind of the way it was here at The Pit—you just made yourself at home.

The heavy scent from inside the kitchen assaulted me immediately upon walking through the double doors. It was Saturday, otherwise known as Menudo Day at the restaurant. While I was a fan of Mexican food—having

Carmen to thank for that—I was not much of menudo aficionado. It was essentially a traditional soup made up of tripe and hominy. I tried to breathe with my mouth open, but exhaled as soon as Amelia took notice of me. I didn't want to offend her, as I knew their menudo had to be just about as fantastic as any of the other dishes they served. It was simply a matter of "it's not you, it's me" kind of situation. After a few seconds, my senses adjusted to the smell and I was okay.

"Wyatt! Didn't think we'd be seeing you again so soon. Not with Carmen at home to cook for you," Amelia said.

My flushed cheeks gave me away and I'm sure she took full notice of my apparent embarrassment upon being found out. She knew as well as I did that if Carmen didn't feed me, it was because I was being punished. "Let's just say I had to fend for myself this morning."

"I see," she said, knowing full well the scope of Carmen's wrath.

"Do you know if Natalie will be around later?" I asked, casually changing the subject. I really didn't want Amelia to know I was smitten with her niece—I know, it was an old fashioned kind of sentiment, but in this case, it seemed appropriate. Damn it, I was smitten, and that was the real reason I came here to begin with so I might as well own up to it, even if it was just for my benefit.

Amelia, bless her heart, didn't make mention of my obvious interest in her niece. "You know, I'm not sure. I bet if she gets hungry enough, or gets bored over at the house, she'll find her way over."

Trying to change the subject again, before she teased me about my crush, I thought back to last night and the owl. Amelia was known around town as the authority on birds. She always kept their lawn at home peppered with bird seed in the hopes of catching some rare bird on its southern migratory path to Mexico. Even the local newspaper did a piece on her (Queen of the Hummingbirds was the headline). "Hey, you're familiar with the different birds around here. What do you know about large owls?"

"What do you want to know?" she asked.

"I was driving home last night from the river and one almost hit my windshield."

She shook her head in disagreement. "Not possible. Owls just don't fly toward moving vehicles."

"That's the thing, it wasn't just any owl. It was a large one with eyes that looked almost human. Like it was taunting me. Daring me to hit it."

This time, Amelia stopped cold. "Had to be a *lechuza*," Amelia said with finality, shaking her head as she spoke.

"Lettuce?" My Spanish wasn't all that great, but I knew enough to know that what I saw last night on the road wasn't projectile produce, although I was sure my Spanish was just rusty.

"No, not *lechuga*, a *lechuza*," she corrected, emphasizing the 'z' as she said it.

"Oh," I said, feeling stupid. When Amelia didn't say anything more, I prompted her for more. "So what is it?"

"I'll tell you, although I don't like to talk about such dark things. What you saw may have been an evil witch in disguise. Legend has it that those that partake in black *brujería* often sell their souls to the devil. *Brujas* like that often shift into owls." She stopped long enough to see if there was any sort of recognition. "Didn't your mother ever tell you bedtime stories?"

As soon as the words came out of her mouth, I could tell she instantly regretted saying them. Sure, my mother, the town drunk, capable of tucking her kid in bed at night. That in itself was a tall tale. Besides, stories about a shape-shifting owl didn't sound like an appropriate bedtime story to me. "No, she was always...busy, you know that," I said. "The owl I saw last night, you're saying it was a witch?"

"A witch, yes," she whispered as she made the sign of the cross. "Most likely a *bruja negra*," she confirmed, more to herself than for my benefit. "A black witch."

It was enough to humor Carmen and the De Leóns when it came to their healing persuasions and spells, but witches? Even though I knew with certainly that witches didn't exist, especially those that can shape-shift into owls, hearing Amelia's explanation I felt somewhat better. If it *was* a witch who could change into the form of an owl, I found that theory much less unsettling than a mutant bird for some reason. That or I could chalk it up to a drunken overactive imagination on my part.

"*¿Qué le dices a ese pobre?*" Ester asked, coming in from the dining room, arms carrying empty plates.

"Wyatt was attacked by a big bird," her sister replied, eyebrows raised.

"You were attacked by Big Bird?" Ester asked confused. "*Como los* Muppets?"

I almost broke out laughing, but didn't out of respect for Ester. Sometimes she got lost in translation and almost always took things too literally. "No, I wasn't attacked by Big Bird or any other bird. My eyes must have been playing tricks on me, that's all," I said.

"Then what do you think you saw out there on the road?" Amelia asked. "A minute ago you sure certain it was a large owl."

"I don't know exactly. I thought I saw an owl trying to bash my windshield last night on my way home, but I could be wrong," I said. I didn't want to make a big deal about it now, especially after Amelia's reaction to the story.

Ester treated the story just as serious as her sister Amelia had. "Owls are *no bueno*. Our *abuelita* used to throw anything away that had an owl on it. Even if it was a gift," she said. "Years ago, our *tío* got her some beautiful owl salt and pepper shakers for her birthday and she tossed them in the trash. *¿Te recuerdas* Amelia?"

"Yeah, I remember," she said to her Ester.

"Why?" I asked. "I thought it was a just Mexican legend." I raised my eyebrows back at Amelia.

Caldero was only a hop, skip, and a jump away—which by Texas standards meant a few hours, depending on how fast you were driving—from the Mexican border, so our town was no stranger to legends and folklore. The story of *La Llorona* was famous in most, if not all, small Texas towns. According to the story, the wailing woman roamed the nearest body of water, crying for the children she herself drowned in order to capture the heart of a prominent man. Then there was the classic story of the school bus full of children who had been hit by a train in San Antonio. Legend has it, if you sprinkle baby power on the trunk of your car and park it in neutral right before you cross the tracks, the ghosts of the dead children will push it safely across; their tiny hand prints captured in the powder.

Amelia just shrugged in response. "Our grandmother grew up in Mexico and even after she settled here, up until till the day she died, she believed them big old barn owls were really vengeful old women in disguise," she explained.

"I was probably just tired driving home last night," I said, trying to convince myself more for my sake than the sisters. I was beginning to believe that it was all just a hallucination on my part. It was a rather late night and maybe the few beers I had hadn't worn off by the time I headed back to the house. For all I knew, it could have been easily explained; like a plastic bag floating in the wind for example.

She gave me another one of her skeptical looks before she went back to stirring the pot. "Why don't you go find yourself a table and I'll get you something to eat. Chorizo and eggs?" Amelia asked, already knowing it was my favorite. It was exactly what Carmen had prepared for me this morning before tossing it in the trash.

I gave her my best smile. "You know it."

Excusing myself to the two De León sisters to grab a table, I walked out and literally bumped into Natalie as she was coming in. She looked like she was deep in thought and hadn't noticed me exit the kitchen. I'd sideswiped her on my way out, as she was on her way in. I was momentarily stunned by the sheer height of her. I figured she was tall, the way she was able to stretch her legs underneath the booth, but I hadn't really given it much thought as she had been sitting down when I first met her, but the woman in front of me now was statuesque, almost godlike, standing almost six-foot tall—it was a pretty safe guess considering I'm six-foot-two. I wondered what it would be like to kiss someone without having to bend down to meet her lips. I then started to wonder what else we could do together besides kiss, but quickly found my voice before she could sense what I was thinking.

"Hey, I came by to see you," I said, hoping I didn't come off as sounding desperate. "You should have come to the river last night. It was a lot of fun."

"Oh, I did. It was the only way I could get my aunts off my case. They thought I was being rude to you last night."

"You were there?" How did I miss her? "Why didn't you say hi?"

"You looked pretty occupied." She tugged on the hem of her shorts, which was either a nervous habit she'd developed over the years, or she was self-conscious about the fact that her shorts were way too short for her Amazonian-like long legs. "Didn't look like you wanted to be bothered," she said.

Shit. So that was the rustling sound I had heard. She must have seen Kelsey and I kissing out on the river. I was just starting to get to know Natalie and there I go and blow it by rekindling old flames that weren't even worth kindling to begin with. "Oh, that. She's my—"

Natalie stopped fidgeting with her shorts long enough to put her hand up, waving the thought away. "No explanations necessary. It's okay, really."

" —my ex-girlfriend," I finished saying.

Her eyes narrowed. "Kind of a weird way to end things, don't you think?"

I shrugged, not knowing why I felt the need to clarify. "We broke-up a few years ago before we went away to school. Guess we just got caught up in the moment."

She seemed to consider that and decided to let it go. "Were you on your way out?"

"Actually, I came by to see you but you weren't here. But now that you are, I was wondering what you were up to today."

"Right now, I'm hoping to get a breakfast taco." Her eyes traveled in the direction of the kitchen. "Care to join me?" She obviously didn't give my brief dalliance with Kelsey a second thought if she was inviting me to join her for breakfast. It was either a good sign or a bad one.

The De León sisters were known for a lot of things, but they were renowned for their breakfast tacos. Not a morning went by without them baking enough tacos to feed an army (even on Menudo Saturday). Back in high school, we used to place orders for pick-up before we headed off to school. First period teachers turned a blind eye to the "no eating in class" rule when it came to a De León breakfast taco. It was considered a sacrilege to even consider having us throw them away if caught. Even the faculty was known to scarf down a taco in the teacher's lounge well before the first bell rang.

After Carmen's refusal to feed me this morning, my stomach greedily grumbled in response. Even if I *had* had breakfast at home, you never refused a De León breakfast taco. Ever. "Absolutely."

"Okay, I'll go and tell the *tías* while you grab us a table. How do you like yours?"

"I already gave your aunts my order. Chorizo and egg."

"Great. I'll grab both our orders then and bring them out if you'll find us a spot to sit."

Ten minutes later, Natalie joined me at the booth with with our food. Now, like I said before, these weren't just ordinary breakfast tacos; the two tacos that lay before us on the table were a work of art. The tortilla alone was the size of a tire rim that took two hands to hold. Just one breakfast taco was substantial enough in nutritional value and calories to cover breakfast, lunch, and dinner.

"So what brings you to Caldero?" I asked between mouthfuls of egg and sausage. Since she appeared to be more sociable, maybe she'd be more forthcoming about herself than she had been the previous night.

Natalie hesitated a second before answering. "Well, as you know, I'm staying with my aunts for the summer. My parents decided I needed to spend some time with them. You know, with them getting on in years."

"Your aunts are great." I knew them well enough to know they were pretty decent for two old ladies. Despite Carmen's expertise in our kitchen at home, I'd spent a lot of time here at the The Pit over the years.

"They're actually my great-aunts. They can be pretty strict sometimes, but it could be worse, my folks could have sent me to my other relatives in Saltillo."

In all the years I'd known the De León sisters, they never given the impression that they were stern, quite the opposite in fact, but I nodded in understanding, although I couldn't really relate. Aside from my mom and Carmen, I didn't have the benefit of an extended family. After my dad skipped out on us, any communication we had with his side of the family was lost. According to my mother, they weren't worth getting to know. The sisters had always treated me like a nephew, or at the very least a distant relation, whenever I came by their restaurant.

"Where exactly are you from anyway?" I asked.

"Well, I was born here, but we moved to Tucson when I was little."

"Ah." I wondered if she would ever come back to visit after the summer was over.

We sat in silence as we ate our massive breakfast. It wasn't one of those uncomfortable silences you often hear about, rather, it was more like a mutual respect for the food in front of us. "So," I started, after it was safe to start the conversation back up again. "Do you always carry those cards around?" I asked, noticing the purple tin she'd set by the edge of the table.

"Sometimes. I like to know what the day will bring."

"There are horoscopes for that, you know," I said in jest.

She laughed, and it was the most engaging laugh I'd ever heard. "Yeah, I suppose so. Do you want me to read your cards?"

In all the time Carmen lived with us, she had never offered to do readings for me or my mother. She always said it was better not knowing what fates await you, which I guess was a polite way of saying, "you don't want to know." When I asked why she did readings for others, she said that some folks needed to hear their futures in order to make peace with their inner demons.

"Sure. What do I have to do?"

"Nothing," she said, shuffling the cards. "I do all the work. This is called a three card spread."

I watched in fascination as Natalie flipped three cards to form a triangle.

She flipped over the top card and laughed. "Fitting. The top card is your present, which is represented by the Page of Coins. This tells me that you are curious and of an inquisitive mind. But we already knew that," she said with a sly grin. "This card here on the bottom left, represents your past and the The Wheel of Fortune indicates that forces beyond your control had a hand in changing your fate. "And this one here." She pointed to the Strength card. "Is your future. You will show great courage through inner strength."

Just as I thought—the cards were nothing more than a parlor trick. You could assign any meaning you wanted. Sure, I asked a lot of questions, but that's normal. As for the Wheel of Fortune card (which closer inspection confirmed *was* Vanna White), anyone who knew me well enough was aware my father ran out on us and my mom drank herself into stupor on a daily basis, not much of a fortuitous fate in my opinion. As for courage and strength, it probably means I'll get dumped by someone soon and get over it.

"What about you? What do your cards say?"

"I already did my reading for the day. Nothing I didn't already know."

"Then why do you read them?"

"In case it tells me something I don't." Her explanation seemed harmless enough and the version of tarot cards she carried around were whimsical and feminine, unlike Carmen's set that were creepy and old.

Breakfast was going well, so I figured I'd strike while the iron was hot. "Say, you want to go out later? Just you and me?" Somehow I didn't think she'd want to get together with the whole gang, especially if she thought Kelsey might make an appearance. Can't say I'd blame her, I didn't want another run-in with her anymore than she did.

"I don't think that's such a good idea."

"Oh, come on. We're eating breakfast now, aren't we? I'd say we're having a good time, right?"

Natalie looked back down at the cards. "I guess, but I have other things to do tonight."

I wasn't going to let her get off that easy. "If you're washing your hair, then what about this afternoon? Surely you don't already have plans."

She laughed at my attempt at humor. "Maybe I already do. You're not the first person to try to, uh, befriend me since I moved into town, you know."

At this early stage, I couldn't tell if she was joking or serious. I was curious if this was just another way of blowing me off or if she really had in fact met someone so quickly. Even though I only just met her the day before, I found myself being jealous at the prospect of her already having someone else in the picture.

"Yeah, sure. Next time then?"

Natalie glanced back at me and I couldn't help but stare into her beautiful eyes. "Maybe."

Seven

I woke up drenched in my own sweat. It either had something to do with the dream I had, or possibly due to the window being cracked overnight. Even in the early morning hour, it had to be about ninety degrees already, a reminder that we were smack dab in the middle of summer. Then again, there were only two seasons in South Texas: hot and hotter. Carmen wasn't going to be happy if she had to keep washing the sheets every time I woke up in a sweat, not to mention letting the air conditioning escape through the open window. From now on I'd have to remember to keep the window closed.

In Texas, Sundays are reserved for family or hunting, that is, if you are able to get out of going to church. Fortunately for me, my mother was hungover most mornings and Carmen attended the ten o'clock Spanish Mass at St. Cecilia's, which usually meant leaving me to my own devices Sunday mornings.

Since I was exempt from going to church and I didn't have a dad to go hunting with, I went over to The Pit for breakfast, making it the second morning in a row. It was the only day of the week where you could get *barbacoa* served with fresh corn tortillas. Every Saturday night, before the De León sisters went to the evening Mass, they would prepare and bury the *barbacoa* in the underground pit they had behind the restaurant, in preparation for the after-church-crowd the following day. It was better if you didn't ask from what part of the cow the tender beef was actually made.

It was only a little after ten, but the place was already packed with holy rollers returning from the varied early morning services. Not only was St. Cecilia's a few blocks away from The Pit, but other denominations were represented within a quarter-mile radius of the town center. Somehow I managed to find an empty two-seater and waited for someone to take my order. Folks waved their hellos and acknowledged my presence, and for the first time, it felt nice to be home. Almost as if I'd never left Caldero.

"Wyatt," Kelsey cooed as she walked past my table. Her parents were already ahead of her, trying to find a table. "Why don't you join us?"

The last thing I wanted to do was spend my morning with the Powers family, especially if I got lucky enough to run into Natalie again. If I agreed to sit with the Powers, that would only lead Natalie to think Kelsey and I were still an item. It was the second time in a twenty-four hour period I regretted doing anything with Kelsey that night at the river. "That's okay, I'm good."

Kelsey proceeded to purse her lips into the pout she was famous for. I'd obviously embarrassed her in front of her parents. "That's silly. You're here all alone and there's enough room at the table for one more," she said, gently pulling my arm.

I brushed her hand off. "Really, it's fine. I don't plan on staying long."

Kelsey did a good job of pretending my words didn't sting, but I knew I'd pissed her off and she was above begging. If I didn't want to join her and her family, she wasn't going to cause a scene in front of her parents. But I knew I'd pay for it at some point, one way or another. She was quite skilled at holding grudges. "Suit yourself. See you around."

I heard a voice behind me. "That looked uncomfortable."

"Natalie, hey. Care to join me?" Never mind I just rebuffed Kelsey and would never hear the end of it from her. I'd just add that to the litany of offenses I'd already committed against Kelsey in the span of minutes.

"If it means pissing her off," she nodded towards Kelsey, who at this point was already shooting eye daggers at Natalie. "I'd love to."

"What do you have against her, anyway?" It wasn't a fair question, especially after Natalie witnessed us making out (and more) out on the river but I asked because I was generally interested. This was something guys would never understand: why women were always at odd with each other. There's probably some sociological explanation or something.

"Let's just say, she's the one that has a problem with me," Natalie said.

Now we were going in circles—apparently they both had a problem with each other. It's no wonder I never got the dynamics between women. It always seemed to me like one was pitted against the other over trivial things. "Fair enough."

"So, what brings you here this early? I kinda pegged you as a late riser," she said.

"Your aunts' *barbacoa* of course."

"Don't you have someone to cook for you at home?"

"If you mean my mom's hair-of-the-dog morning concoctions, you'd be mistaken. Besides, Carmen's at church and doesn't cook Sunday mornings. It's her day off." Or rather, it was her day off taking care of the McKenna family. Carmen usually spent the day doing headings and readings. She once told me that performing her rituals on the holiest days made for better results. Ever since I was a kid, there was an unspoken agreement that we'd stay out of Carmen's way on Sundays.

There wasn't much to say after that. After my attempts to get Natalie to engage in anything other than breakfast small-talk, I had nothing. "So..."

"So..." she replied back, feeling the awkwardness between us. "Do you want to hear your reading for today?"

"Sure, why not?" I only hoped Kelsey and her family weren't still eying us. They weren't Catholic (lapsed like me or otherwise) as my family was raised, but Baptist, which was worse in this particular scenario, viewing anything involving magic or mystical as the work of the devil. I'm sure the Vatican's official stance on tarot readings or anything having to do with *curanderismo* wasn't exactly favorable, but for the most part, it was just simply frowned upon by the local parish, especially since the practice had elements that stemmed from Catholicism.

Natalie pulled out the purple tin containing her tarot cards. She shuffled the cards like a pro and handed the stack to me. "Cut them," she instructed.

I did my best to cut the deck in half and placed the bottom stack over the top as she instructed. I didn't believe in any of this, but I knew it meant something to Natalie so I played along for the fun of it. Though if Carmen knew I was having my cards read, I knew she'd be furious. She always kept me in the dark about all her *curandera* stuff. I asked her about it once and she said that it was better not knowing what the future holds. "It's fine for others who need to hear," she had said, "but you must experience life for yourself."

Natalie looked serious as she concentrated on the cards in front of her. She looked so at ease and confident in what she was doing, I could sit and watch her do that for hours. While she didn't say a word in those few moments, I could tell she was deep in thought, her mind buzzing with images and the meanings behind them.

She finally flipped the first card. "You've been dreaming about something. The Seven of Cups tells me that your dreams are likely to become reality if you believe in them."

My jaw almost fell. How in the world did she know about the dreams I'd been having? I didn't even have a grasp on them myself, always forgetting the moment I woke up. I didn't say a word and let her continue the reading. I tried to keep a blank expression so she wouldn't notice my surprise over the card's meaning.

"This one here," she said, tapping the left card, "your past, is the Eight of Coins, which means you enjoy the repetition of things in order to perfect your skills."

It was a boring card if you asked me. Her explanation could have meant a number of things. Like I've said before, you could pretty much assign any meaning to fortune telling, but I wasn't going to voice my opinion on the matter. I was just grateful this one didn't have anything to do with my dreams. I wasn't sure if what she was telling me was actually real or if I was actually starting to believe. Either way, it still freaked me out a little.

"Oh," she said, turning over the final card. "This one isn't a very good future I'm afraid. This one tells me you will soon be defeated or rejected."

I glanced at the card bearing a woman in a cloak and dagger outfit holding five swords with a solemn man in the background. Even after what was said about my present card, this one didn't bother me as much because I knew exactly how to interpret that one. "Hey, do you want to go out tonight?" I asked suddenly, already knowing how she would respond.

"I don't think that's a good idea."

"Ha! See? I've already been rejected and it's only," I said glancing at my watch, "ten-thirty."

Natalie laughed. "See? I told you. You never know what your future holds until you consult the cards."

"Well, isn't this cute?" Kelsey walked up to our table as Natalie gathered up the cards she set aside while we ate our breakfast. "Looks like y'all are having a good time. What are those, tarot cards?" She asked, peering down at the table. "You know, you shouldn't mess around with those things. My mom said they do nothing but bring the devil closer."

I actually knew for a fact that Mrs. Powers went to see Carmen from time to time. My guess was to find out whether or not Mr. Powers was having an affair (which he was) and what she could do to keep him from straying (which she couldn't). But I wasn't going to tell Kelsey this, not with her folks a couple tables away.

"It's just harmless fun, Kels," I said, defending Natalie, who for the most part, just ignored Kelsey.

"Just don't come crying to me when you fall under a witch's spell," she said, emphasizing the word witch, knowing full well what she actually meant. I looked over at Natalie and shrugged. I knew it was a bad idea for us to sit together while Kelsey was around, but I was enjoying every second I spent with Natalie, so in the end, I didn't really care much what Kelsey thought.

Kelsey went to join her parents at the cash register, where they were paying the bill. "See you around," she said on her way out.

"Sorry if I'm messing things up between you two," Natalie said, looking not the least bit sorry about the exchange.

"I told you, there's nothing between us. We dated in high school, that's all."

She shrugged it off and stared down at the table. "Do you really think that?"

"What? That we aren't getting back together? I told you, that's all in the past."

"No, what you told Kelsey. That this is all just for fun?" She held up the purple tin that contained her tarot cards.

The last thing I wanted to do was make fun of her and I certainly didn't want her to think that's what I was doing now. "No, that's not it at all. Carmen, the woman who raised me, does readings. Not that she's ever done a reading for me or anything. I guess I just don't know enough about it. I'm sorry if I hurt your feelings."

"That's okay. I understand."

In a move that surprised even myself, I slid my hand across the table in an effort to hold her hand. Knowing exactly what I was about to do, she pulled hers away. "Sorry," I mumbled. For trying to hold her hand, for allowing her to think I was making fun of her—for lots of things. I'd only known her a couple of days and I was already apologizing for things.

"I'm going to see if they need any help in the kitchen," she said abruptly, rising quickly from her seat.

"Yeah, sure. And the offer to meet up later is still on the table."

"I'll keep that in mind," she said, already walking toward the kitchen door, leaving me to ponder just what exactly I had done wrong.

"Don't give up on her, sugar. She'll come around." Amelia appeared by my side as if by magic. It was kind of irksome the way she always seemed to appear when I was in a moment of weakness. I didn't even notice her come out of the kitchen as I watched Natalie head in that direction. Or perhaps she'd been in the dining room taking orders and overheard our conversation. In either event, it was embarrassing to be shot down yet again, especially in front of her aunt.

"What's the deal with your niece anyway?" I figured if anyone knew, it would be one of her aunts.

"She's always been reserved, even as a child," she said. "Just give her time. She'll come around."

"Somehow I doubt it, but I'll try." I wasn't entirely convinced, but I took Amelia's advice to heart. With Natalie ditching me, I decided it was time to head home or maybe see if Tyler wanted to get together. Since I was here, I might as well make the most of it and spend time with my best friend. Anything to get Natalie out of my mind for awhile. I still wasn't sure why I was so determined to get to know her, but there was something pulling me toward her. It was the same eerie pull I felt in the pit my stomach that brought me back to Caldero.

"Why don't you come over for Sunday dinner tonight? Ester and I never have any company over anymore. Ester and I used to have ourselves a grand ol' time when we were youngsters. The stories I could tell you," she hooted.

"Well, anyways, it'd be nice to have some young folk over for a change. Do two old women a favor and join us this evening," Amelia said.

One of the best things about the restaurant was that the sisters never kept regular hours. The doors never closed until the last customer was served, even if it meant staying open until ten o'clock or later, with the exception of Sundays, when they always closed at five.

Not one to miss an opportunity to see Natalie again, I accepted. "Thank you for the invite, Amelia. I'd love to come over."

She seemed pleased I accepted her invitation. "See you at seven sharp."

Eight

I was beginning to have reservations about all of this. I had no idea what possessed me to come home for the entire summer. Yes, I do. It was those damn dreams and the burning in my gut urging me to return. But after all that prodding, what was the point? I didn't even have the luxury of spending time with the only family member I had, let alone one who meant a damn to me—my mother. Sure, it was nice being cared for by Carmen who loved and was as good to me as any mother, and it was nice catching up with Tyler and the others, but there were only so many times you could go to the local bar and reminisce about the glory days. So why was I here?

Like now. A couple hours after my late breakfast, I ran into Tyler just as he was headed over to Hector's

Lounge for their famous happy hour specials (daily from 1-4pm, open seven days a week). With nothing better to do with my time until I had to get ready for dinner at the De León's, I joined him.

"So," Tyler started to say as I caught up to him, "what's up with you and that new chick in town?"

"Heard about that already, huh?" I said, keeping the details short. Not that there was much to report, but the less I spoke about Natalie the better. I was afraid if I showed too much interest, Tyler might wonder what all the fuss is about and go after her himself.

I was rewarded with an elbow nudge to the chest. "Just let me know how that turns out for you. Cuz when, and, believe me brother, *when* she shoots you down, I'm making my move."

No surprises there. He really wasn't kidding, but I really couldn't hold it against him. That's just the way he was. I often admired his self-confidence, especially when it came to women. But in all seriousness, I figured that if I didn't have a chance with Natalie, nobody did, and that included Tyler, so I had nothing to worry about. "Yeah, I'd like to see that."

Tyler looked behind me and smiled. "Well, if you don't mind, I think I'll take my shot now. Because look what the cat dragged in," he said, nodding at the entrance of the bar.

It was Natalie, and while Hector's usually attracted a varied crowd, I somehow didn't figure her the type to frequent a place like this. Her choice of watering holes wasn't the only thing that was off about her, though. She had gone from her standard cut-off shorts and t-shirts she was wearing earlier this morning—a look I'd grown to like —to looking like the unfortunate victim of a bubble gum factory explosion.

Natalie was head to toe in bright pink, from the plastic headband she wore, down to her flats. If you squinted, it looked like a flamingo had set foot in the bar. Not that she looked bad, I'm sure a lot of guys go for that conservative preppy look, but it just didn't fit the Natalie I was getting to know.

"Here," Tyler gestured, "come sit with us."

"Thanks," she said. Natalie hopped on the bar stool, being mindful of the shortness of her dress. Due to her extreme height, I assumed anything she wore verged on the skimpy side. As she adjusted herself on the stool, she smiled at the two of us before motioning to the bartender, "I'll have a bourbon, top shelf. Two fingers, straight up."

Upon closer inspection, I noticed she was wearing pearl earrings almost the size of golf balls. What was it with her and this new look? Then it dawned on me—she had probably attended the late mass over at St. Cecilia's after breakfast. The get-up was probably Amelia's doing. Surely that had to be the reason. The way I saw it, anyone deserved a stiff drink after one of Father Hilario's homilies —from what I remembered as a child, he tended to get long-winded.

Again, I was struck by how much I had misjudged her. Not that you should judge a book by its cover, but still. The Natalie I had breakfast with seemed more like someone who enjoyed a cold beer on a hot summer day— or even a nice glass of chilled white wine—than the bourbon-straight-up kind of girl that sat next to me now. I guess there was a lot I still had to learn about Natalie.

"Is this town always so dead?" she asked after placing her drink order.

"What you see is what you get," Tyler responded, obviously making his play. "I'm sure if we put our heads together, we can make the most out of this one-horse town."

Natalie pursed her lips together and considered his offer. "I like what I see so far. What about parties? You guys like to party, don't you?"

Tyler took her latter comment as an invitation to continue flirting. "You know what they say, the smaller the town, the bigger the party. I'm sure something could be arranged."

She took a long sip of the bourbon the bartender had placed in front of her and considered it. "It might be worth checking out. Keep me posted."

While there were certainly a lot of women that would find Tyler charming and irresistible, it took me by surprise that Natalie would, too. I wasn't jealous—okay, maybe I was a little—it was more than that. She just didn't seem like the same Natalie I met a few days ago at The Pit. There was definitely something not right about the way she was acting and carrying on.

I continued to watch Natalie drink the remainder of her bourbon without so much as a grimace and slapped the glass back down on the bar. "This was fun and all, but I'm gonna bail," she said, hopping off the stool. "I'll see you two around?"

Hadn't her aunts informed her about dinner tonight? Knowing how much she resisted any kind of attempt to spend time together, and how she was carrying on with Tyler, I didn't want to have my invitation revoked, or worse yet, have her invite him over for dinner as well, so I didn't mention it. "You bet."

She flashed me a winning smile before giving us each a peck on the cheek as she made her way out of the bar. "Can't wait."

No, not like Natalie at all.

Nine

Now, I'd known the De León sisters since forever and had frequented The Pit since I was old enough to crawl, but I'd never been formally invited to their house. Even though I knew Carmen was as close as anyone could really be with the sisters, and as social as the De León sisters were, I don't think anyone has ever been asked to visit them in their home—or to hear Amelia tell it, not in decades. If anyone was taking notes, this would be something to go down in the record books.

My family wasn't wealthy by any stretch of the imagination, and the huge Greek Revival my mother and I lived in was passed down to her, being the only relative still alive to inherit, along with the meager trust. So while we lived in one of the nicer parts of town—which was in all actuality a joke considering how small a town Caldero actually was and didn't really have a bad part of town—I was still nervous about going to dinner at the infamous De León house.

To call it a house was an understatement. Unlike ours, theirs was a grand Queen Anne Victorian, built a few decades after the homes in my own neighborhood. Despite its impressive stature, the house was slowly fading from the outside; its once bright purple hue now a muted, cracked lavender. If you asked the folks around town, no one could tell you exactly how the sisters came into such a property, but there was plenty of speculation as to how they could afford to maintain such an imposing structure. Their restaurant did reasonably well, if you judged by the sheer number of customers on any given day, but not enough for a place this grand, even if the house was declining in its old age. The whole town knew about the sisters' side business, but much like their low prices on their menu, they hardly charged their clients at all for cleansings and readings. It was hard to imagine them earning a large enough income to support what little upkeep they could afford on a house like theirs.

And as much as the residents of Caldero loved the sisters, it didn't stop them from speculating as to how they came upon a house such as theirs:

"Had to be an inheritance."

"I heard they had an uncle in Mexico that was worth a fortune and left them everything."

"Amelia was secretly married to some millionaire from New York..."

"...someone told me the Yankee husband mysteriously died."

"It's not really their house."

"They're witches."

It was the latter of the conclusions about the De León sisters finances that was always discussed in hushed tones and behind closed doors. While it was no secret the sisters served as faith healers to the community, there was a big difference between a practicing *curandera* and a full-fledged witch, according to them. For to consider yourself a true witch, or *bruja*, one was aligned with the devil or other such dark forces, while being a spiritual faith healer was harmless. At least that's what the good God-fearing folk in this town believed.

One would think sisters would be shunned for having such a reputation, especially in a place like Caldero, but it was quite the opposite in fact. The sisters were well-respected, and aside from the curious nature surrounding what was considered to be a small fortune, no one who had ever used their services had the nerve to cross them. As far as I was concerned, that was the real power they held over the town—they knew everyone's secrets.

I thought of this as I walked up the long walkway toward the house. Perhaps the the real question should be, what secrets did the sisters have of their own?

As much as I was looking forward to dinner and seeing Natalie, I hesitated a second before knocking on the massive brass knocker. It was overwhelming, being perhaps the only person in recent years to be invited over to the De León's for dinner, while at the same time trying to impress their niece. I was nervous on both counts. It would make for an interesting evening.

After what seemed like forever, the door finally opened. It was Natalie. I was hoping for one of the sisters to greet me at the door so I still had the element of surprise before Natalie figured out what was going on. Gone was the pink, preppy, prissy outfit from earlier today, replaced with her standard uniform of standard cut-off shorts and a t-shirt. It was the same outfit she had been wearing during breakfast. Not that I minded when women got dressed up, but in Natalie's case, seeing her dressed like this, the way she was now, made her a little more approachable.

"Wyatt, what are you doing here? You can't be here," she hissed. I could tell by just by the expression on her face that not only had her aunts not cleared the guest list with her, but, just as I suspected earlier, avoided telling her all together about having company over for dinner.

"Why not? Your aunts invited me over." Despite Natalie's reluctance at getting to know me, I sure as hell wasn't going to pass up an evening with the mysterious sisters. Even if she wasn't interested in me, I could at least get a small glimpse of the life that was the De León family. I don't believe anyone in my shoes would turn down the opportunity.

She still looked cross. "Well, they shouldn't have."

I just didn't get it. Her aunts were going out of their way to make sure Natalie made the best out of her time here and she was doing everything in her power to fight them. "Why can't we just be friends? Do you have better things to do?" I asked.

Natalie just stood there and said nothing.

Standing outside arguing my way for a dinner invite was embarrassing, even if I was expected. "What gives? I've done nothing but try to be your friend and you keep brushing me off. I thought we had a good time earlier today. You seemed to finally be making an effort to make friends around here."

"Breakfast was fun, but—" Natalie started, but I cut her off.

"No, earlier this afternoon. At Hector's. Ring any bells? You stopped by after church."

Natalie blanched at what I was saying. "Church? This afternoon?"

"Yeah, the late mass," I said, confused. "Isn't that why you were all dolled up?"

It was clear to me the registered look of shock on her face meant she had no idea what I was talking about. "I'm sorry, but I think it's best if you left. My aunts had no right inviting friends over without talking to me first."

"Ah, so we are friends."

"That's not what I meant."

"What then? Explain it to me." She wasn't going to get rid of me that easily. And what was up with the sudden memory loss? She only had that one glass of bourbon, which certainly wasn't enough to cause a blackout. There was a lot she wasn't saying and I wished she would just come out and say what was bothering her.

She sighed and continue to support herself against the door, reluctant to let me pass. "It's not that simple, Wyatt. You don't want to get involved with someone like me, trust me. Nothing good ever comes out of it."

"Someone like you?"

"Just go home and forget about dinner tonight. Forget about me," she said. "It's better that way."

I heard what she said, but her eyes said something different entirely. "You know what I think? I don't really think you mean it. You're going to have say something better than that if you want me to go away."

"Wyatt is that you?" I could hear Ester calling from inside the house. "Natalia, let the *pobre* in before the *vecinos* start to talk."

Presented with two options—I could stay or I could go—I decided I wasn't going to let Natalie win this one. She could turn down my advances, but I knew she wouldn't go up against her aunts. No one was brave enough to do that, not even a stubborn niece.

"Yeah. You wouldn't want the neighbors to talk," I said as I pushed the door open and brushed past her to greet Ester. "Thank you for the dinner invitation, Ester. Whatever it is y'all are cooking, it smells delicious as always."

Defeated and outnumbered, Natalie closed the door and followed me into the dining room where the aunts had already set the table for supper. There was nothing she could do or say at this point without offending her aunts. I knew it, and she knew it. It was a small victory for me, even if I did gain entry into Natalie's secret world by way of Amelia and Ester.

"We're so glad you could make it," said Amelia, smug with pleasure over winning this round against Natalie. I'm sure she overheard our conversation. "We were so worried Natalia wouldn't make any friends here. It's nice to see y'all getting along."

Natalie just sat there being stubborn and didn't say a word. That was fine by me. Two could play at that game. "Famously. In fact, after dinner, Natalie and I are going down to the river."

I could feel the cold hard glare from across the table. My announcement was obviously a surprise to Natalie, but she played it cool and didn't say anything in front of her aunts. She didn't have to: it was quite clear by the expression on her face she was beyond pissed.

"That's nice," Ester said, pleased they were making some headway filling up their niece's social calendar.

"Isn't it?" I grinned. As much as I hated taking advantage of the situation, it was kind of fun. The way she continued to stare at me told me she was somewhat curious about our outing later that evening, even if she wasn't happy about it. "Now ladies, you must tell me what that amazing smell is."

"It's gumbo," answered Amelia, lifting the lid off the pot. Any other hostess would have transferred the dish into a tureen, not the old cast iron pot in which the meal had been cooked. I guess the sisters didn't care much for formalities. "Old man Hockaday shot himself some doves today, and graciously donated some for tonight's supper."

"I thought dove season didn't start until Labor Day?"

"We don't ask questions when accepting gifts," Amelia responded. "Besides, you know how Old Man Hockaday is. At his age, he doesn't give two hoots about the game wardens and besides, he thinks because he hunts on his own land he's immune to whatever the penalties are for hunting off-season."

"Well, it smells delicious." I was a sucker Louisiana regional cuisine. I added a heaping helping of gumbo over the white rice already served on my plate and took a greedy bite. I was pleased to find that it was creole, rather than cajun style gumbo (cajuns use lard, or oil, as a base for their roux). You gotta love the French influence in their gluttonous approach to using butter. I was embarrassed to admit to being somewhat of a "foodie," which could be a direct result of being spoiled by one of the best cooks in the world—Carmen. I savored the warm blend of tomato and spices; Hockaday's dove was also an added bonus.

"I just hope our gumbo compares to the kind you get over in New Orleans," Amelia said.

"This probably by far the best gumbo I've ever had," I said, between mouthfuls, meaning every word, and savoring each bite. "Is it a family recipe?"

"*Ay dios mío,* no," said Ester. In the South, it was considered bad form to poach someone else's recipe without giving proper credit.

"No dear, an old friend of ours passed it on, only after promising we would never divulge her secret ingredients," Amelia explained.

The secret ingredient was probably an extra stick of butter. "Well, I'm honored you thought enough of me to make it tonight."

"Now that the cooks have been complimented, let's finish eating so we can go," Natalie said, obviously annoyed that I seemed to be enjoying myself.

I ignored Natalie. "I'm almost afraid to ask what's for dessert." Clearly I was enjoying myself, even if she wasn't. I was ashamed to admit that I was having fun at Natalie's expense.

Ester beamed, proud to be able to offer her hungry dinner guest something for dessert. "*Tres Leches*."

I think I died and went to heaven that evening.

Ten

At Natalie's urging, we skipped dessert in favor of going to the river before it got dark, only after she promised I could take some of Ester's cake home with me after I dropped her off.

"That was pretty low, what you did back there at dinner," Natalie said. "You knew I wouldn't be able to get out of going out with you if you mentioned it to them."

She was right and I didn't deny it. I knew how much her aunts wanted their niece to get out of the house and I took advantage of the situation. "Oh come on, I promise I don't bite."

Dealing with Natalie was somewhat like a challenge. I liked challenges. Maybe that's why I was so insistent on being with her. But unlike the sweet victory of success one felt after tackling most obstacles, I had a feeling I wouldn't be losing interest anytime soon. There was a reason I was so drawn to her. Only I wasn't sure what that was just yet.

"You just don't get it do you?" Natalie sat with her arms crossed in the cab of my truck, still reluctant to go anywhere with me. I still didn't understand why, but she was in my truck and we were headed to the river. It was another small victory for me.

"No, I guess I don't. Why don't you explain it to me?"

"I already told you, it's not that simple."

She was as stubborn as a mule, but she had met her match. "That's okay, I'm pretty good at figuring out complex things. People say I'm a pretty smart guy. I got accepted into med school, remember?"

"And you're going back in a couple of months," she pointed out. "What then?"

"What does that have to do with anything?" Then I realized what she was getting at. Here I was, trying to start a relationship and at the end of the summer I'd be going back to Tulane while she remained here or went back to wherever it was she came from. Why didn't I think of that before? No wonder she didn't want to get involved. She didn't want to get hurt.

"I know what you're thinking and it's not that."

"How do you know what I'm thinking?"

"Look, I just don't want to burden you with my problems when you're just going to end up leaving, that's all."

"What problems could you possibly have? I'm the one with baggage remember? My dad left me and my mom when I was ten and my mom's a raging alcoholic."

"If only I had those kinds of problems," she said, instantly regretting them as soon as the words came out of her mouth. "I'm sorry, I didn't mean it that way."

"It's okay. I know you didn't."

We got to the place where I wanted to take her. After a few minutes of walking, it didn't take long for us to get to my favorite spot along the Guadalupe, further down on the opposite side of the river from where I'd partied with the others the first night I was back in town. It was more secluded than the other areas along the river. This is where I used to go to when my mom slowly began her downhill battle with alcohol. It was the place my dad used to take me tubing when I was little and fishing when I was old enough to hold a pole properly. For once I didn't have to say a word. Natalie would understand how special this place was to me.

And she did. "It's beautiful, Wyatt. Do you come here a lot?"

I grinned. "I thought you might like it. Haven't been back here in years," I said, pleased she appreciated the beauty and solitude of my special place.

Natalie sat down near the river's edge and stared at the rippling water. "I'm sorry I gave you a hard time back at the house. I just don't understand why you're so determined that we be friends. And even if we were friends, that's all it would be."

On the surface, what she said made sense. She didn't want a relationship with someone who was just in town for the summer, fine. But I wasn't sold. I didn't even know her, but there was something about her that made me want to reach out to her. In the short time I'd known her, I couldn't get her out of my mind. It's like there was this energy that was determined to put us together no matter how hard she resisted. "Okay. But I don't understand why you're so against us being friends."

"I told you already, it's complicated."

This constant back and forth between us was teetering on the verge of ridiculous. "It's always complicated, Natalie. Spin me another tale, but don't tell me it's complicated." Now I was beginning to wonder if all this is even worth the trouble. Maybe she was right, I was going back to Tulane in August, my time would be better spent hanging out with Tyler and the others.

"You just don't get it. And you wouldn't understand if I told you."

"You keep saying that, yet you haven't taken the time to try. I might surprise you."

She thought about it for a moment. "Okay, fine. I'll make a deal with you. If I decide to make an effort to be friends, do you promise not to bring up anything I don't want to talk about?"

It didn't seem like I had a choice in the matter, especially if I wanted to keep seeing Natalie, so I caved. "Deal. So, do we shake hands or what?" Somehow I didn't think suggesting sealing the deal with a kiss would go over too well.

She stuck her hand out to meet mine. "Deal."

"Now that we're friends, a few of us are planning to go to Caldero's Dance Hall on Friday. Do you want to come? Just as friends, of course," I added before she could protest. "You'd have to save a dance for me of course, and I promise I won't step on your feet."

"I know I'm going to regret this, but screw it, I'm game. You're right, there's only so much you can do around this town and I'm sure as hell bored. But don't think for a second I'm considering it a date."

☾

By the time I arrived home—my rather large piece of *tres leches* cake wrapped in foil as promised—I had finally got the opportunity I had been waiting for— dreading, really, this whole time since returning home. My mother.

She was lying on the couch in the living room, staring at a picture of my father. If my mother hadn't stuck to the same script over the years, I'd think it was a bad case of déjà vu. I had hoped she had given up that little ritual by now.

"Wyatt," she said, surprised by my presence. "When did you get home?"

"Just now."

"Why didn't I know you were home? How long have you been back in town?" she slurred.

It dawned on me that my mother had no idea that I had been home for several days. It was my mistake in assuming she was referring to me returning home for the evening. She was in worse shape than I thought if she only just acknowledged that I was home for the summer. I knew Carmen had in fact told her of my arrival, so the booze must have dulled her memory.

"Mom, I've been home for days now. Didn't Carmen tell you?"

Her vacant stare spoke volumes. She had no recollection of any such conversation with Carmen. "No. She didn't tell me. Why wouldn't she tell me?"

"She did, Mom." I sighed, waiting for the exasperating conversation that was about to take place. "You just don't remember."

This was a prime example of the ongoing battle with my mother. It was always a case of her not being told about something or people purposely keeping secrets from her. That was all part of the paranoia that went on in her mind, fueled by the booze. Only there was no grand conspiracy, just the disorganized thoughts of an inebriated mind. I couldn't even begin to recall all the times she had forgotten to pick me up from school or celebrate my birthday. To hear her tell it, every reminder of a forgotten memory or event was an attack against her.

"That's ridiculous. Of course I would remember being told my son was coming home," she insisted. "I'm going to talk to Carmen first thing in the morning about this. How could she not tell me?"

"No, Mom, she did. You've been drunk the entire time I've been here and you're drunk now."

As polluted as she was by all the liquor she'd consumed, she still apparently had feelings. Tears began to form and ran down the sides of her cheeks. Perhaps there was something still alive inside of the shell that was once my mother. But whatever emotion I had invoked a second ago quickly turned into anger.

"Is that how you speak to your mother now? Is that what that school of yours teaches you? To be an inconsiderate son?"

There was no way I was going to win this argument, not in her condition, so as much as I wanted to spend time with my mother, I decided to call it a night. It's not like she was really there anyway. "I'm turning in. We can talk about it tomorrow." I doubt there would be a follow-up conversation—she'd probably forget about this, too.

By then she had already returned to staring at the photograph of my father. She had tuned me out, oblivious to me still standing there.

Eleven

It was Friday night, time for everyone to head out to Caldero Dance Hall. The name wasn't very original, but that's the way it was done in the Lone Star State. Some of the oldest historic dance halls were named after they towns they were established: Cherry Springs in Cherry Springs (1889), Gruene Hall in Gruene (1878), Kendalia Halle in Kendalia (1903), Luckenbach in Luckenbach (1887), and well, you get the idea.

One could say the new the owners of the dance hall, Kiki and Chris, were an oddly matched couple. According to the rumor mill (they were hardly ever wrong with a seventy-five percent accuracy rate), Kiki was a former stripper (somewhere near Eagle Pass) and Chris, a former DEA agent. When they bought out the dance hall several years back, we all had our suspicions that they were running from something—or someone. Kiki always seemed to be out of place in her skimpy outfits and body glitter but determined to make the best of it, and Chris seemed too young to have already retired from law enforcement.

And it wasn't necessarily Kiki's former career as a stripper that made her a social pariah around town—body glitter notwithstanding—it was the fact that she and Chris weren't married, yet lived together. In Caldero, that spoke volumes in a town with a large population of residents over fifty—and none of it good.

But that didn't stop the townsfolk from going to the dance hall on date night for a little dance and twirl. I knew Natalie said it wasn't a date, but in my mind, I was going to treat it as one. I would pick her up at the door promptly at eight, open doors for her, and even pay for her drinks. I only hoped she wouldn't give me a lecture on women's lib. Despite my mother's failed attempts at being a good role model, I'd be damned if folks around town thought she didn't raise a proper son, even if it was mostly Carmen's doing.

The evening started innocently enough, with me picking up Natalie at her aunts' house. As I drove on the worn caliche drive to the main house, I could feel the nervousness beginning to set in. I wasn't sure why I was so nervous, but maybe it was my subconscious telling me to turn back and forget the entire night's plans.

Since this time around Natalie was well aware I'd actually be coming by the house, I wasn't expecting one of her aunts to open the door. Natalie didn't strike me as the kind to fuss over what she was going to wear, so I was a little surprised she left me waiting in the foyer with her aging aunts as we tried to make small talk.

"Wyatt! We are so happy you are taking Natalia out tonight with your friends," Amelia said, ushering me in the house. "We don't know what you said that made her agree to it, and we don't want to know, but thank you just the same."

A thunderous storm of footsteps, announcing Natalie's descent down the stairs, could be heard all the way into the living room, where the sisters had insisted on offering me a cocktail while I waited.

"God, you make me sound like a leper," Natalie said, walking into the room.

Amelia stared at her niece. "No. You manage that all on your own by refusing to make friends." She stopped talking long enough to inspect her niece's standard attire of cutoff jean shorts and t-shirt. "I thought you two were going dancing? I hope you haven't changed your mind and allowed this nice young man to come around here for nothing," she said.

"I'm still going. And don't expect me to go back upstairs and change," Natalie said, pulling on a long piece of thread hanging from her cutoffs and twisting it around her finger.

I thought she looked great for a night of dancing. Even though she'd stuck to her uniform of shorts and a t-shirt, she made an effort by trading in her flip-flops for cowboy boots. But kept my opinions to myself. It wasn't a date, remember? "I promise I'll have her home early," I assured Amelia. Although from what I'd gathered of the situation, Amelia probably didn't care one way or the other as long as her niece went out and had a good time for a change.

Natalie's aunt just smiled. "My niece staying out late is the least of my concerns," she said. "Now, you two go on and have fun."

As we got in my truck and took off, my nerves began to set in again. "You sure you're cool with this?"

I could see Natalie nodding out of the corner of my eye. "Sure, why not? Besides, like I said before, it's not like this is a date or anything."

"Whatever you say," I said. Even though she didn't dress up for the occasion, I still couldn't help but consider it a date. I mean, that was the whole point of going to Caldero's. Dancing to the slow rhythm of the music, with the mixture of sweat and spilt beer serving as an artificial pheromone, stirring up dormant hormones, was the reason couples flocked to the place on Friday nights. To get their groove on—in more ways than one.

"Well, I intend on having you stick to that promise," she said. "I only agreed to go out tonight because I couldn't stand another night with my aunts. They mean well, but one more game of gin rummy and I'll scream."

"You mean you guys play with cards other than tarot?" I laughed.

"Funny."

We drove with the windows rolled down and the smell of fresh-cut grass filled the inside of the truck. It was one of the things I missed about living in Texas. The scent of sweet cut grass after a rain and the sweet musty smell of hay bales after a harvest was a far cry from New Orleans, with its gardenia-blanketed nights masked by the stale stench of beer and vomit wafting off the French Quarter pavement from Mardis Gras past.

"You're awfully quiet," she said. "Normally you're talking my ear off."

"Just thinking."

"About what?"

"How much I missed this place."

"Then why'd you leave? There are plenty of good colleges here you could have gone to," she pointed out.

"Oh, I don't know. To get away from my mom. Start over. Why do most people go away to school?"

"I wouldn't know. I've never went to college."

That was kind of a shocker. Just from the short time I'd known her, she'd always given me the impression she was not only street smart, but book smart. "Really?"

"Nope. Didn't even fill out the application."

"You never thought about going to college?"

"Not especially. My life is kinda complicated that way."

There was that word again—complicated. "Yeah, I'm starting to figure that out," I said, dropping the issue of college. I didn't want to her to feel like I was judging her. Perhaps her family didn't have the means to send her to school. If that was the case, I didn't want to bring up a sore subject.

"So, tell me about the place we're going."

"Caldero Dance Hall. And there's not much to tell really, other than it's one of the oldest dance halls in Texas. The owners a somewhat of an odd lot, but good people."

"Is this what all the cool cats do around here on a Friday night?" she asked, clearly not impressed, judging by her sarcasm.

"Aside from hanging out at the river? I guess, but it's actually a lot of fun. There's not a whole lot of places around here that offer live music and buckets of dollar beers."

"Gotcha."

What I told Natalie was true. You'd be pretty hard pressed to find a venue within a sixty mile radius that not only had a decent line-up, but aside from cheap beer, with Kiki and Chris as the new owners, they also allowed you to bring your own cooler. And as luck would have it, one of my favorite bands was playing tonight. I'd seen them play over a dozen times over the years, but it was always more fun when they played more intimate settings like this one.

Pulling into the parking lot, I noticed everyone had arrived at the same time. I had hoped Natalie and I would be among the first to show up, so as not to make a big deal of our non-date, but it looked like introductions were going to be made en masse.

"Hi, Wyatt." Kelsey was the first to approach us and I only prayed she would be on her best behavior. I may have dated her once upon a time, but that didn't necessarily mean I was blinded by her true nature. She was still forever the queen bee she had been in high school, and acted every bit the nasty bitch that was expected of her. Admittedly, I'd pretty much excused her behavior back then, which I now regret, and I had a feeling she hadn't grown much as a person these last few years. I only hoped the drones wouldn't pay too much attention to Kelsey and would get to know Natalie on their own terms.

To her credit, Kelsey didn't say a word about me bringing Natalie, but I didn't expect the pleasantries to last. We all flashed our ID's at the door and found a prime spot near the small wooden platform stage. So far, no one, especially the other girls, said anything offensive in front of Natalie. Not that I expected them to, but with Kelsey present, there was no telling whether she'd already poisoned the hive with gossip.

Once the band started to play, the couples at our table got up and went out on the dance floor. I offered Natalie a beer from my cooler and we were content to watch them from the sidelines. As I admired the couples on the dance floor, I noticed an elderly couple a few tables down and I envied them for a moment. They must have been in their seventies, yet here they were on a Friday night, drinking beer and enjoying themselves in their best pressed jeans and matching cowboy shirts.

"So do you want to dance?" I extended my hand out to Natalie, praying she wouldn't shoot me down in front of the others still seated at our table.

"Sure, why not?"

She allowed me to lead her onto the dance floor. I wrapped my arm around Natalie, my hand settling against her waist, and I clasped my other hand around hers, pressing it up against my chest. Within moments it was clear Natalie was an experienced dancer. She followed my lead effortlessly, as if we'd been dancing for years.

To call it dancing was to put it mildly. It was more of a rhythmic slide across the worn wooden floor planks than an actual dance. The Texas two-step was an art form that was often imitated, but could never be replicated, not in any other part of the country. There was a subtle finesse to the dance. One didn't just step to a two-beat count. You caressed the floor with your feet just as you would run a finger against your partner's flesh. If done right, the soles of your boots get so worn that by summer's end, there's a hole right where the balls of your feet have shuffled against the ground.

The music scene in New Orleans, however, was a different experience altogether. I'd gone to Tipitina's and a few other joints a few times over the years when I wasn't studying or working, and there, the dancing seemed decadent and indulgent, much like everything in New Orleans, as opposed to slow and purposeful.

No doubt my friends would laugh to hear me describe it this way, but instinctively they'd know it to be true or they wouldn't be taking their dates dancing to begin with, and a places like Caldero's would have closed down decades ago. In an age where folks always seem to be in such a hurry, even in a small town like Caldero, weekends at the dance hall allow for the often underrated (mistakenly so) pleasures of foreplay.

Tyler must have thought so too, even if it was on a subconscious level, as he was already on his third dance partner of the evening. I wondered who'd end up being the lucky girl to take him home at the end of the night.

I twirled Natalie as was customary at the end of a song and we went back to the others. The band was taking a fifteen minute break, replaced by music from the overhead speakers; a Tejano number I'd never heard of. The few couples that got on the dance floor twirled and bounced, reminding me of those quick step routines you see on *Dancing with the Stars* (my roommate Paul was a fan). I took that opportunity to grab us a bucket of beer, having already run out of what I'd brought from home.

The rest of the evening went with Kelsey keeping her distance from Natalie and vice-versa. I didn't know if it was because she was embarrassed at being bested at her own game, or because she didn't want to show just how vindictive she could be in front of witnesses. Regardless of the reason, it suited me just fine, as all I wanted to do was spend a pleasant, non-drama-filled evening with Natalie.

Soon, the bucket stopped replenishing itself, which signaled the end of the evening. The evening ended with one last song by the band and I grabbed Natalie's hand without bothering to ask for the last dance of the evening.

Not to be left disappointed by evening's end, the band began to play an old fan favorite, as couples made their way onto the dance floor. It was always the last song of the evening, even if the band wasn't there to perform it live. We were creatures of habit I realized, as everyone danced and sang along to the lyrics. Nothing had changed in the years I'd been away. Caldero Dance Hall, along with every other place else in this town, was like a living time capsule.

"Can I cut in?" It was Kelsey and she looked determined to ruin what had so far been a perfect night. It was a power play and it was one she wasn't going to win this time around. For years, Kelsey had been successful in getting her way, but not this time.

"I'd rather not," Natalie said. I was glad she was on the same page. Neither of us were willing to give into Kelsey's adolescent behavior.

"Wyatt?" Only, what Kelsey really was saying was, "Are you going to let her speak to me like that?"

I wasn't about to let Kelsey spoil our evening, so I gracefully maneuvered Natalie further along the dance floor, but not without saying, "Get over it, Kels."

In the end, I'd considered the night a success. No one gave Natalie any trouble, aside from Kelsey, and I felt like were were getting to know each other a little better—even if she didn't consider it a date. My concern was that Kelsey wasn't going to let go of what happened and would spend the remainder of the summer making Natalie's time here in town a living hell. In that respect, the night could be chalked up to a prelude to something disastrous this way comes.

We didn't say anything the last few minutes it took to get to her house and we didn't have to. It was one of those comfortable silences—the other type of silence you also hear people talk about. I wondered if it meant anything at all.

I finally rolled into the driveway parked in front of the house, cutting the headlights as I didn't want to wake the sisters. Still, not a word passed between the two of us as we sat in the truck and I wondered if she was thinking the same thing I was.

It turned out, she was. "I had a great time tonight, Wyatt."

"I did too. Too bad it wasn't a date."

"Why's that?"

"Because then we could end it properly."

"What? Like with a goodnight kiss? Look Wyatt, I already told you— "

"Who said anything about a kiss goodnight?" Although that's exactly what I had been thinking. "I just meant that if this were a real date, I'd be a gentleman and walk you to the door. Since it's not, we'll just have to say our goodbyes here."

Natalie laughed. "Well in that case, goodnight."

I leaned over her to unlock the door—I could still be a gentleman, even if I wasn't walking her to the front door —just as she reached for the door handle. "Goodnight, Natalie."

She kept her hand on the door handle and stopped. She turned to face me and leaned in, coming an inch from my face. "On second thought," she said before kissing me.

It was everything I imagined it being and I didn't hold back—who knew when I'd get another opportunity to be this close to her. I grabbed her neck, pulling her that much closer to me, as our lips remained pressed against each other. She didn't resist, allowing me the chance to devour the sweet taste of her mouth for as long as she'd let me.

When we finally broke apart, I had to ask. "Not that I'm complaining, but what changed your mind?"

"Nothing. I just felt like it," she said. "Now, don't get any ideas. Remember, this wasn't a date."

I grinned in spite of her words, still dizzy either from the beer I'd consumed earlier or the kiss that still lingered on my lips. "So you keep reminding me. Hey, will I be seeing you tomorrow night at Ty's?"

"What's going on at Ty's?"

"He's throwing a party remember?"

The blank look on her face told me she had completely forgotten about the party Tyler was throwing in her honor, but she then said, "Oh, yeah sure, I remember. It sounds like fun."

And with that, she hopped out of the truck's cab and ran all the way up to her house.

Twelve

As promised, Tyler was able to throw together a party at the last minute. Although around these parts, it wasn't all that hard to do. Just mention free beer and the folks will come. It was like my grandpa (before he passed away, leaving me his beat-up old Ford) always said, "There are only two types of beer: free beer and cold beer."

Not once did I ever associate my social drinking habits with my mother's own debilitating struggle with alcoholism. I always attributed her drinking to my father leaving us, grieving in the only way she knew how. Me, I grieved in a different way. I kept a near perfect GPA in high school, I studied to the point of exhaustion in college, I worked hard to save every dime I could. Those were all things I could control. Yes, I enjoyed a cold beer on occasion, even something a little stronger when warranted, but I vowed at an early age never to be like her.

I wasn't really up for a party, but it seemed to mean a lot to Tyler to host one in honor of Natalie, despite her disinterest in him. Last night only confirmed I was making some sort of progress with her. "Dude, you know she's not into you right?" I finally asked him as he hauled the last of the kegs onto the back porch of his house. His parents had gone to Austin for a long weekend, so for him it was yet another perfect excuse to let loose.

"Noted. I saw the way you two were at it out on the dance floor last night," he said. "But hey, any excuse to party, right?" For all his faults, Tyler was always optimistic.

I grinned. "Right." You couldn't argue with logic like that. In a way, I was happy he had decided to throw the party even though it was clear Natalie wasn't as interested in him as she had first let on back at Hector's. But for Tyler, a lost prospect opens doors for new ones. There were plenty of girls coming to the party tonight and Tyler knew he had his pick of the willing and able. As for myself, I'd take any opportunity to hang out with Natalie. Provided she showed up, that is. And after that kiss we shared last night, I had my doubts as to whether she'd show up at all.

As podunk of a town as Caldero was, everyone still understood the concept of being fashionably late. The party was set to start at sunset—which was around eight-thirty—but folks didn't start arriving until well past nine o'clock. Unlike the rest of the world, the fine residents of Caldero adhered to a different concept of time. It was like living in the Land of Mañana. Things moved at such a snail's pace that even the clocks were slow.

Once the party was in full swing, I did my best not to look around for Natalie. I'd only be that much more disappointed if she didn't show up and I didn't want to make a big deal out of it, especially in front of Tyler. In short, I didn't want to look like a fool. So instead, I focused on catching up with old friends and I managed to forget Natalie for a moment.

But there was someone who did manage to make an appearance and she was headed straight in my direction. I sincerely hoped there were no hard feelings after what happened last night on the dance floor. I'd publicly humiliated her in front of our friends and broken a second cardinal rule: don't ever cross Kelsey.

She made her way through the crowd in her confidant swagger and approached me. "I've been thinking about it and I've decided to forgive you," Kelsey announced.

"For what? Last I checked, you're the only one that needs to be forgiven," I said.

"For hanging out with that girl Natalie. But never mind that, you're right, I'm sorry," she said, not sounding very apologetic at all. "Friends again?"

I almost burst out laughing. It was so typical of Kelsey to offer a truce as phony as her hair color. Even after all this time, she never seemed to get the bigger picture—that those around her weren't so daft we couldn't see her for who she truly was. I doubted very much her intentions for a reconciliation, but it wasn't worth the trouble fighting with her. It was better to just pretend we were friends and leave it at that. If I smoothed things over with her, she'd cause less trouble in the long run. "Sure. Truce."

"Great! Where is she anyway? Aren't you two like joined at the hip?"

I wish. "No, it's not like that and to answer your question, I don't even know if she's coming over or not."

"Trouble in paradise already?" She tried to hide her smug smile but wasn't doing a very good job.

"I thought you were going to make an effort to be nice?"

"No, I said we could stay friends," she said. I wasn't budging on the matter and she knew it. "Oh all right, I'll make an effort. And just to prove what a good sport I am, I'll even grab your new girlfriend a drink."

"Huh? I just said I wasn't sure—"

Kelsey nodded in the direction behind me. "Seems she decided to make an appearance after all. Now if you'll excuse me, I'll go see about getting her that drink."

I didn't want to appear too eager to see her, not wanting to give Kelsey more ammo in her arsenal to use against me later, so I hung back and let Natalie come to me. It turned out I didn't have to avoid her that long before she found her way over to where I was standing.

"You weren't kidding, this is some party," she said.

I gave her a stupid grin in response, happy she was here. After the way we ended things last night, I wasn't sure if she would spend the rest of the summer avoiding me or not. Women were fickle that way—especially after they give you a glimpse into their vulnerable side. "Glad you decided to drop by. Tyler is known for his wild parties."

It was shortly after ten o'clock and it hadn't taken some of the guys long to get drunk. One guy—I think it was Mike Pearce—who had graduated a year ahead of me, was already passed out on the couch with his empty red plastic cup lying at his feet. I think I heard someone mention he was already married with two kids and another on the way. Perhaps starting the evening doing a keg stand to prove he "still had it" wasn't one of his brighter ideas.

"You'd think y'all would have gotten it out of your system back in high school," she said, nodding over in Mike's direction. As usual, she was always candid about what she was thinking. She wasn't the least bit impressed by the party that was thrown just for her. And I liked that about her. It was refreshing to be around a woman who was honest and wasn't afraid to speak her mind.

"Ah, but now we've evolved into dumb adults trying desperately to turn back the clock. But all jokes aside, I guess when you get us all together like this we can act pretty immature. Old habits die hard I guess." I said.

I didn't think Kelsey was actually serious when she said she'd get a drink for Natalie, but there she was, sauntering toward us with two red Solo cups in each hand. "Hi, Natalie. Didn't think we'd be seeing you tonight," she said in a voice that was tad higher than her normal pitch. "And to show what a good sport I am about last night, I brought you a beer."

Natalie narrowed her eyes as she looked at the offering in Kelsey's hand. "How nice," she said, with just the right hint of sarcasm in her tone, "but no thanks."

Kelsey scoffed. "Oh, come on. It's a party," she said. "Besides, it's not like I roofied it or anything." She smiled at Natalie, extending the drink for her to take as if it were a dare.

Not wanting to back down from a challenge, she took the beer from Kelsey's hand. "Thanks."

"You're welcome. Now, if you'll excuse me." Kelsey brushed past us, making a beeline for the cluster of girls ahead, formerly known as the Caldero High School varsity cheerleading team.

If I were to tell my friends back in New Orleans about everything that went on during my summer here, they'd find it peculiar. Not the partying or hanging out on the river, but the fact that everyone I knew from back then was in town. The thing is, it wasn't so much that everyone just happened to be in Caldero for the summer. The truth of the matter was, no one ever left. Even those who went away to college were only on temporary leave. They eventually came back.

Natalie glanced at the cup in her hand and then back at me. "She seems to have done a one-eighty after what happened last night at the dance hall," she said. "What'd you say to her?"

"Nothing, but I'd play it safe if I were you. I can go grab you another beer if you want, I wouldn't put it past her if she *had* put something in your drink," I said.

She laughed. "No, it's okay, trust me, I'm willing to risk it. Bottoms up," she said and raised her cup full of beer before taking a sip. "I could be wrong, but if you ask me, I think she's jealous."

It was my turn to laugh. "Jealous? That's one word I've never heard used to describe Kelsey." Normally it was the other way around with women being jealous of Kelsey. "Vindictive, yes. Controlling, check, but jealous? Nah, not Kels."

"Guys can be so dense sometimes. How can you not know when a woman is envious of another woman? Think about it. You two used to date in high school, and from what I saw the other night at the river, you guys obviously had a pretty hot and heavy relationship. Not only that, but you take the new girl, me, out dancing, who ends up humiliating her in front of you and her friends. You're a smart guy Wyatt, connect the dots, she's jealous."

"If you say so." Still, something wasn't right about Kelsey's behavior tonight and I don't think it had anything to do with being jealous, because that would imply Kelsey was capable of real human emotions. If I were a betting man—and I was known to be from time to time—I'd say she was out for revenge. "Watch your back just in case," I said.

The evening was going about as well as I could hope for. Natalie hardly left my side and we were finally making headway, at least in my mind—she laughed at my jokes, flirtatious attempts by other guys were rebuffed, and she even casually held on to my arm. At one point she even held my hand as we maneuvered our way to the back deck.

Then everything took a turn for the strange and unexplained. After a few hours, I began to notice a change in Natalie's behavior. It was subtle at first—talking more than usual, sliding her hand up my thigh as we sat, switching from beer to liquor. I began to have my suspicions.

But nothing could have prepared me for what she wanted to do next. "Come on, let's go find a spare room," she said. Everyone who's ever been to a party knew what that meant.

As a red-blooded-American male, I made it a point never to refuse a proposition like that, but I knew something wasn't right with her proposition. "And do what exactly?"

"You know," she said with a smile, her head tilting toward the upstairs bedrooms.

"How many beers have you had? Not that I'm refusing or anything, but this isn't really like you, Natalie."

She laughed, but it felt wrong—not like Natalie at all. "You don't know me well enough to make that claim, cowboy." She pulled me close to her body and whispered in my ear. "Don't you think it's about time we got to know each other a little better?"

"Why don't we go back outside and get some fresh air?"

Natalie pushed me away. "Look, if you're not interested, just say so. There are plenty of guys here that have been giving me *the look* all night. Do you know that look, Wyatt? I'm sure you do. Just like I'm sure any one of those guys wouldn't hesitate to give me a tour of the house."

"I'm thinking maybe Kelsey *did* put something in your drink," I said. "Please, let's go outside. Clear your head. Then I can take you home."

She shook her head vehemently. "I'm having too much of a good time. You can go home if you want. Don't let me keep you."

I couldn't stand to be around her this way, and as much as it pained me to leave her there, I took her advice and left.

Thirteen

More than a week later, I still felt miserable over the incident at Tyler's party. Call it stubbornness, but it was more likely a case of the cowards. I tried my best to avoid Natalie those last few days. I didn't know what I expected of her and I didn't know if I should even expect anything of her. She made it perfectly clear that we were just friends, so I decided to give her the space she so clearly desired.

There was literally nothing to do around here, so to kill time, I spent the week catching up with Tyler, and when I grew weary of him rehash every play by play of his college football career, I spent some quality time with Carmen. I even learned how to cook some of her favorite regional dishes from Mexico. Anything to distract myself from going over to Natalie's house to demand an explanation. I didn't even bother to ask Tyler what happened after I left the party—partly because I didn't want to know. They say ignorance is bliss, but it to me it felt like I was in one of Dante's nine circles of hell.

It infuriated me that I cared so much about someone I knew so little about. She was quite insistent that under no uncertain terms we would ever get involved, but she flat-out refused to tell me why that was. I could live with being rejected, just not the secrecy behind it all.

Only I knew I couldn't hide from her all summer. Frankly, the town wasn't big enough to play hide-and-go-seek. It was inevitable that at some point I would run into Natalie around town and have to face what was happening —or not happening—between us, so in the end, after a week of sulking in my own stew, I decided to place myself one step ahead of fate and go see her myself.

If I was expecting an apology, I didn't get one.

"What are you doing here?" As per usual, she blocked herself between the door frame and the door, indicating I wasn't welcomed in her home. I thought we had gotten past that when I went over for dinner, but I guess ditching her at the party was cause to rescind my invitation—like they did with vampires on that TV show.

"Can't a friend come by to see another friend?"

"Not after the way you treated me the other night at Tyler's party they don't." She was obviously just as pissed as I was. Maybe more. It never occurred to me until just then that perhaps she had been avoiding me too.

"The way I treated you? Are you seriously that much in denial? Have I ever been anything other than a perfect gentleman around you? If you felt that I pushed you too hard or made you uncomfortable just say it, but if anyone was being inappropriate that night it was you."

"You just left me there," she accused. "I woke up all alone at Tyler's and had to explain to my tías why I came straggling home at six in the morning. You call that being a gentleman?"

I couldn't believe what I was hearing. Yes, I regretted leaving her there in the first place, but she'd left me no choice. I didn't want to be a party to her lewd behavior and do something we'd both come to regret later. This was not to say I wasn't sexually attracted to her, because I was, but I didn't want her that way—drunk. The way I saw it, she was the one out of line that night, not me. God only knows what she was doing and with whom to warrant staying there until dawn. "You're right, I did leave you there, but only because you weren't being yourself."

"What the hell are you talking about, Wyatt? All I remember was drinking a few beers and having a good time. The next thing I know I'm waking up on some stranger's couch."

"Tyler isn't exactly a stranger." In the times I had been with Tyler this past week, he made no mention of

Natalie waking up on his couch. Did something happen between them? Were they both trying to hide something? Even if Tyler and I were best friends, blood brothers even, there were some lines you just didn't cross.

"He's a stranger to me. I was so embarrassed, I left as soon as I could before he found me there."

That explained why he didn't tell me, there was nothing on his end to tell, but it didn't explain what had happened that night. Did she end up shacking up with someone or not? When I left, she hadn't seemed drunk enough to pass out in someone's living room. Now I felt terrible for leaving her there all alone without knowing anyone. "You seem to do that a lot."

Natalie was seething with anger at this point. "Are you calling me a whore now?"

This conversation was certainly not what I had in mind when I came by to see her. "No. That's not what I meant. It's your memory, Natalie. You seem to forget a lot of things lately." I was starting to get worried about her sudden gaps in her memory. I wondered if she suffered from some medical condition she didn't yet know about.

In that instant her anger was replaced with fear. "Oh, God. It's started."

"Are you okay? What's started? Natalie, are you sick?" That would certainly explain her odd behavior and resistance in getting involved.

"Can we go to your special place? We need to talk."

"Let's go."

Fourteen

I was so preoccupied with my thoughts about Natalie that not two minutes after we began to walk down the river's path, I tripped over a large tree root, gashing my knee. Embarrassed, I sat down on the offending root to assess the damage. It hurt like hell, but I didn't want Natalie to notice how much pain I was in.

"Wyatt, are you okay?"

I gently lifted the torn part of my jeans and took a look at what appeared to be a serious cut that ran across my knee. Blood was running down my my leg, ruining my good pair of jeans even more. The wound was going to require stitches, and knowing that pained me more than the actual injury itself. "Yeah, I'm okay, but I'm gonna need stitches."

Natalie came over to take a look for herself. "Let's see."

"I'm fine," I said, obscuring the wound from her view. It was a pretty deep cut and I didn't know if she was the squeamish type. Hell, I was the one going to med school and the sight even freaked me out.

She dropped to her knees and brushed my arm aside so she could get a better look at my leg. "Come on, it can't be that bad."

"See? It's nothing," I said, waving her off. "But I guess we better get back. I'll have to go to the doctor to take care of it."

But Natalie didn't move. She continued to rip the torn portion of my jeans, widening the gap in order to have a better view. She hesitated upon looking at the wound, but then, in a move that surprised me, she covered the injury with the palm of her hand, pressing it gently. I instinctively winced, thinking it would hurt like hell, but amazingly, it didn't.

After a few seconds, she removed her hand and inspected the wound again. "I think you'll live," she said.

There was still blood caked on my skin where the injury was, only the injury was gone. What the hell did she do to me? "If I had my doubts about you before, I don't anymore. I know there's something you're not telling me. What did you do?" Instinctively I moved away from her, causing her to flinch at my reaction. I was ashamed to

admit it, but at that moment, I was afraid of her. Men weren't supposed to be frightened of the opposite sex, but no one could have predicted a scenario like this.

"I think I need to head back to the house," I said. Since meeting Natalie that first day at the restaurant, I didn't want to be around her.

She avoided eye contact with me. "Sure, I understand."

I'd hurt her feelings, but I didn't care.

We rode back into town in silence and I didn't say a word as I dropped her off on the way to my own. I didn't know what to say.

☾

I didn't even stop to say hello to Carmen when I finally made my way back to the house. I went straight up to my room and replayed the events over and over again in my head. What the hell did she do to me? Was this the secret she'd been keeping from me? Why she fought so hard not to be friends?

I refused to look at my leg because if I looked at it, I would have to come to terms with what just happened back there at the river. It was something I didn't want to try to understand. What Natalie did defied everything I had learned about the human body.

As I considered the possible logical explanations to what just happened, a memory resurfaced. I'd been healed like that before—by Carmen. It was a childhood memory I'd repressed, as it didn't hold any significance, until now. As a kid, I was always getting into mischief and like most little boys, I got hurt on occasion. Once time, I'd trespassed into Old Hockaday's farm and fell climbing down one of the trees on his property, spraining my wrist in the process. It wasn't that serious an injury, but to a ten-year-old boy, the pain was enough to teach me a lesson and keep me from trespassing (for about a month). I remember my mother kissing the boo-boo before Carmen tended to my swollen wrist and by the next day, the injury was gone. I always assumed later it wasn't a sprain to begin with, but now I was beginning to have a twinge of doubt.

Looking back, there wasn't a time I could recall when I was ever really sick. Every cough only lasted a day, every fever dropped within minutes, and every injury healed within moments—just like that day I fell out of the tree. I tried to come up with a time when I was ever sick and I couldn't. Was I some kind of medical marvel or were there other powers at play?

I finally looked down at the ripped portion of my jeans and inspected the wound that should have been underneath all that denim. The dried blood had taken on a dark ruddy hue by now, the only evidence that there had ever been an injury. That alone what proof of something, but I of what I wasn't sure.

Part of wanting to be a doctor was to find answers for things that couldn't be explained; seeking solutions for problems that confounded others. Was I being close-minded simply because I was confronted with a situation I didn't want to explore or even consider?

As far as I was concerned, my healed injury wasn't proof of anything, yet—but it was enough for me to go back to Natalie to demand some type of explanation. I was resolved to at least hear Natalie out. I wasn't as afraid of her now as much as I was about what she had to say.

Driving back to the De León's, I ran over all the possibilities in my mind and came up empty. I couldn't come up with a reason why I never got sick as a child, nor could I explain why my leg miraculously healed just by Natalie's touch. I was hoping that if I went over there Natalie would be able to fill in the gaps.

It was as if she was already waiting for me. She sat on the worn wicker loveseat on the front porch. I wondered if she'd been sitting here the whole time, while I was back home struggling with my own thoughts.

"Let's go around back," she said. "We can take a walk."

The back yard, if you can call it that, was a small spread of land and it was just as run down as the rest of the property. I could tell someone came by on a weekly basis to mow around the main house, but the rest of the grounds remained overgrown by brush.

"I'm sorry I sprung all that that on you," she said.

"What was it you did back there?"

She shrugged. "I healed you."

"Why? And how?"

"I guess you can say I'm like a *curandera*. When you brought up my memory loss, I realized that it was only right to tell you, which is why I had you take me to the river, but then you hurt your leg, so I thought I'd just show you instead."

Despite hurting her feelings even more than I already have, I smirked at what she just revealed. There was a monumental difference between telling people you could heal their souls and what Natalie just performed on my leg. "It still doesn't explain what happened back there. Besides, I thought *curanderas* only performed things like faith healings? I knew you were into all that superstitious stuff, but I didn't actually think you took it that seriously."

She didn't take offense to my words. "That's where you're wrong. I'm not talking about superstitions, folklore, and myth, Wyatt. I'm talking about *real* magic. Powers you couldn't even begin to understand."

"I don't understand the difference." Didn't Carmen and the De León sisters perform a type of magic? If they didn't, why would half the town go to tend to their ailments, mend their souls, and heal their broken hearts?

Not that I'm a believer in such things, but real magic? I never voiced my opinions to Carmen because she seemed to enjoy her calling of helping others, and besides, who was I to judge?

"No, I imagine you wouldn't. There's a fine line between faith, magic, and the supernatural. In my world, the line is blurred. Take my aunts, for example. They openly practice *curanderismo*, which is just another name for a faith healer. They heal the afflicted, both externally and internally, but it's all mind over matter. There's really nothing supernatural about being a *curandera*. It's really just a smokescreen to cover what they actually are. Their cover works because the clients tend to believe in the power behind the faith. At the same time, there are true healers, which is something else altogether, and that's where the line gets blurred. And at the end of the day, we're not even talking about magic, like casting spells from a book. It's something more powerful than that. I'm talking about real honest to goodness witches."

"I don't believe in witches." To hear all this was beyond surreal.

"Sure you do. You believe in *curanderas* like Carmen or my aunts."

"The jury's still out on that. I'm not sure I even believe in what they do. Not judging or anything, but I don't see how you can compare it to real witches, you just said it was all smoke and mirrors. But witches? Like the kind with cauldrons and broomsticks? Not that I've changed my position or anything, but how is that different from someone practicing real magic? Hypothetically speaking of course."

"I use the term only in the context that you think it means. I'm just trying to simplify it for you to better understand."

"I still don't get it."

Natalie seemed frustrated, but continued anyway. "Anyone can train, with the right tutelage, to be a healer. It's a practice usually passed down from generation to generation. Every culture in the world has them in one form or another. The abilities I have on the other hand, can't be taught, you're born with them. A gift from a higher power, if you will."

"What are you saying exactly?" She didn't really have to go further, I had a funny feeling what she was about to say next. "Why are you telling me all this?"

She sighed, as if the weight of the world rest upon her. "I guess I'm just tired of keeping secrets. And if we're going to keep hanging out together, I figured I have to tell you the truth. Although I'm not sure how much time you want to spend with me now after what I've just told you."

It was an easy assumption. As soon as she tried to show me what she could do, I'd bailed on her. "Sorry I acted like an ass back there at the river. It's just hard to wrap your mind around, you know?"

"Yeah, I know. And I'm sorry, too. I've been keeping my secret since as long as I can remember. It's not like I know how to tell people about it without freaking them out, so I'm sure it's not easy trying to understand it."

"But a healer? I don't even know what that's supposed to mean, exactly." It was quite a stretch, from calling yourself a folk healer to calling yourself a witch with healing powers. The former indicated you were very spiritual, albeit misguided if you asked me, but the latter implied you were one screw loose away from the nut house.

It was as if she could read my mind. "What I am is not like practicing witchcraft or *curanderismo*," she said. "They're simply practitioners of magic. You'd be hard pressed to find a race or culture that doesn't have some practicing form of the faith. There's a grain of truth in the notion that certain cultures are able to perform magic. The majority of faith practitioners fall into the category of charlatans and con artists, then there are those that use the tools that help them perform a type of magic, but there are a few like me who walk among all cultures and faiths."

"Is there a name for what you are?" I asked.

"There's no true name for what I am, not anymore, but in some circles we're considered Healers, drawing our healing powers from our ancestors. In short, I'm not exactly mortal, I'm a descendant of The Ancient Ones."

This is not what I was expecting her to say, especially since I still didn't even know what the hell she was talking about. Were we still talking about witches or something else entirely? All I know is, I expected her to say something prolific, but nothing like what she was telling me now. "What do you mean you're aren't human?"

She refused to meet my gaze. "It's not that I'm not like you, exactly. I'm just not like regular mortals. I'm different," she explained. "You know, maybe telling you wasn't a very good idea. But I just thought that if I explained it to you, you'd understand why I can't be involved with you. I thought that perhaps if I healed you, maybe you could understand and believe me."

"A healer," I said, repeating what she'd said. Actually, I did remember reading something in my cultural anthropology class about the mythical beings that were touched by God and blessed with the power to heal. "Isn't that just a myth? Ancient beings that were given the ability to heal?" I didn't want to admit that I found the class incredibly boring, so I forgot most of what was said about the healing race of shaman priests. But to hear Natalie tell it made it interesting. I was slowly starting to come around.

A small smile formed on her lips. "You know a lot more than I gave you credit for, college boy. Looks like that education paid off," she laughed. "Yes, there are the myths about mystical beings being able to heal through the power of their touch. There were other cultures too. Either they were not aware of the gifts that had been bestowed upon them, or their stories got lost in translation. In other words, it wasn't limited to isolated societies. Most societies that have a strong belief in spirituality are based on the Healers that lived alongside them. The Native Americans, the African shamans, even the witch doctors. It's all based on truth. The majority are just spiritual healers like *curanderas*, but others hide behind those labels. The true Healers."

"I see." Although, I really didn't. "A healer, huh. Not quite human...just what exactly are you?"

She was thoughtful for a moment, as if she didn't want to continue with the conversation. "Well, since I've already let the cat out of the bag, I guess it wouldn't hurt to explain what I can. At least, what I actually know of my family's history."

This conversation was a little unnerving. "Okay, but you're not going to tell me you're like those wack-ass preachers who can heal you with the power of their touch are you? You know, the kind with all the snakes?"

I didn't mean for it to be, but Natalie thought my comment was funny. "God, no. Those guys give beings like me a bad name." She laughed in spite of herself.

"Good, because that would be a little too freaky for me. I'm all ears then." As if what she'd told me so far wasn't freaky enough.

She continued. "In the beginning, special beings were designated by God to heal humanity. Not only their souls, but the flesh. Very similar to the witch doctors or *curanderas* folks are familiar with today, only this particular race of healers were marked directly from Heaven."

"So, you're more like an angel or something," I said, trying to convince myself that if that was the case, what she was telling me wasn't so bad. I could live with the idea of Natalie being some kind of celestial being.

She shook her head. "My kind are descendants from a very powerful race of healers directed from God, but trust me, we're no angels. In the beginning, there were only The Ancient Ones. But then, they lost sight of their mission here on earth and began to want what other mortals had: love, passion, and, most importantly, free will.

"In the end, they got what they wanted and as a result, those born of the union between them and mortal humans became something else entirely...a whole different race all together. Some call us witches, others demons, while those that still remember remember the stories of The Ancient Ones consider us blessed beings, or even demigods," she laughed. "But make no mistake, we are darkly beings, no matter what you call us."

There was nothing dark about Natalie and I refused to believe she was some kind of evil entity, even if she wasn't a angel. "I wouldn't go as far as to say that. You look pretty angelic to me."

That's when Natalie laughed the most heavenly laugh that contradicted her earlier assessment of herself. She was every bit an angel even if she didn't believe it herself. "If you only knew! Do you know what I had to go through just so I could look normal?"

Of everything she just told me, that statement alone caught me off guard. Forget that she just told me her deepest darkest secret about being some kind of healing witch, but trying to look normal? What exactly did she look like before? My mind raced at the possibilities and I began to envision a pair or wings, a tail, or worse yet, a set of horns.

To demonstrate, she held out her left palm and ran her finger across the scar by her pinkie. "See this? There used to be another finger."

I went from staring at her hand, to her, then back to staring at the scar on her hand. Okay, knowing that she'd once had six fingers on her left hand was kind of irksome, but now it had been reduced to just a faded scar. She didn't have the extra digit anymore, so it really wasn't as bad as she made it out to be. I reminded myself that I was going to be a doctor, I'd be looking at worse things than a congenital hand defect.

"I know, I'm a freak on all sorts of levels," she said, making light of the disclosure. She was obviously embarrassed about her former abnormality.

"Is that normal for…I mean, well, you know what I mean."

She laughed again. "Yeah. Even though we're kind of a watered down version of The Ancient Ones, we still carry most of the original traits. One of the hallmarks of Healers are the little extras, literally. Excess hair, extra fingers, extreme height, you name it."

That explained her long glorious mane of tresses, her unusual height—her overall presence. "When I first met you, I was in awe of your height. Like an Amazonian, only better. And all that comes from upstairs?" I pointed up to the sky for emphasis, not wanting to say the word "heaven." I wasn't sure such a place existed, but it sounded like Natalie was.

Natalie finally looked at me and smiled. "I'll take that as a compliment. But seriously, where do you think supernatural beings come from? If you were to believe in that sort of thing, that is."

I shrugged, not knowing where she was going with this. "I don't know. Never really gave it much thought." *Because they don't exist.* So why would I? Who spends their time pondering about things that aren't real?

Everything I've ever read or heard pertaining to religion I cast aside as myth. If Carmen knew how I really felt about organized religion she'd drag me to church to confess and repent for my sins. I was a man of science, not faith. It was my believe that no one set of ideals was more superior than another. There was no question as to whether or not there was a higher power out there—I just wasn't sure what that meant.

"Gifts like mine were either passed down from either the heavens or the other worlds below. Either way, there is no true black and white. The Ancient Ones who passed on their powers were marked from Heaven, but beings like me were born of human mortals. We still possess the power of free will, just like regular humans, and that in a sense, that allows us to choose."

Now I was even more confused. "Choose what?"

"Whether or not we wish to embrace our gifts or not. It's kind of what got the original healers in trouble in the first place. Choosing to be with the mortals they were meant to heal and protect, to live a life without restraints over all other responsibilities."

I processed the information as best I could under the circumstances and suddenly began to laugh at the absurdity of it all. I believed in modern medicine and evolution, not innate healing powers. But I believed Natalie—I believed that she believed. I was becoming just as illogical as her story for buying into it.

"What's so funny?" Natalie asked.

"This town. Don't you get it?"

"No, what's funny about it?"

"Caldero. I should have caught it sooner. It's not a coincidence that this town is named after the Spanish name for cauldron. Get it? Witches cauldron?"

I didn't quite understand everything I had set out to find, but it was a start.

Fifteen

For a week after she revealed her big secret, we carried on as if everything were normal. I couldn't ignore what I saw with my own eyes and I don't think I could have continued to be with Natalie if I hadn't experienced her healing powers firsthand, but for now, I was happy to simply enjoy her company and she was finally allowing me to take her on a real date.

For as long as I can remember, the Mesquite County Livestock Show and Fair has always been held the second week in March, but this year, they had to push back the date because of unforeseen maintenance work on the fairgrounds due to flooding. It's wasn't an opportune time, as by July, the average temperatures reach into the high nineties, but it was the earliest it could be held this year. I had never participated in the livestock show as a teen, never having been a member of 4-H or the Future Famers of America, but it was always a welcome event nonetheless as the entire school system shuts down for a week, giving everyone a much-needed break during the semester. I was no longer in high school, but the event was still a welcome distraction.

I walked hand in hand with Natalie as we did a long lap around the newly renovated fairgrounds. All the enticing smells I remembered as a kid were still there: funnel cakes, cotton candy, fajita tacos, turkey on a stick, and, my personal favorite, candied apples. I took in a deep breath, savoring each distinct scent as we strolled passed each vendor, and despite the heat, I was secretly glad the show had been pushed back so I could enjoy it this year.

"So what is there to do here?" Natalie asked.

"Whatever we want. We can check out the livestock judging, food entries, or just gorge on all this delicious fair food. And after all that, we can go to the carnival."

She looked at me in mocked amazement. "You're really into all this aren't you? Doesn't seem like your kind of thing."

"Yeah, sure. I mean, I'm not into the whole raising cattle aspect, but coming here reminds me of when I was a kid. It's the kind of memories you don't ever forget. Besides, it's all part of coming home again."

"I guess I can see its appeal."

"And if you're really nice, I might even win you a stuffed animal at the carnival tonight."

Natalie nodded, pretending to be serious. "I'll try to be on my best behavior."

Before hitting the food booths, we decided to go through the barns housing the livestock that were going to be judged throughout the week. Even though I didn't grow up on a farm, I still admired all the animals that were paraded around. The first barn we ventured into was the cattle barn and we were immediately greeted with the sweet smell of hay and cow manure.

"Why is he doing that?" Natalie asked, pointing to a guy wearing a blue corduroy FFA jacket. He was spraying an obscene amount of hairspray on a cow's tail that had been teased to look like a beehive-bouffant.

I shrugged. "Why do girls use hairspray? To make them look good."

"Oh."

"Hey, Wyatt, over here!"

I turned and it was Old Man Hockaday calling us over to his stall. His family bred some of the finest cattle this part of Texas and I think he waited all year in anticipation for the show. I don't think I remember a time when his cattle didn't win some sort of champion prize. Hockaday also took his cattle to the Houston show, but I think he favored this show more, being his home turf and all.

The old man took a swig out of his Coke can, only I had a pretty good idea it wasn't a soft drink he was swilling. Beer and liquor were banned from the show grounds, so the only way around it was to empty a Coke can and refill it with booze before entering the grounds.

"Hi, Mr. Hockaday. Have you met Natalie?"

He gruffed, sizing up Natalie. "You're the De León's niece," he said, taking another sip of whatever was disguised in the drink can.

"Yes sir," she said.

"You expected to place this year?" I asked him. "Mr. Hockaday's nephews are entered this year," I explained to Natalie.

The old man slapped the animal on its hind leg. "This here girl is a champ. We have high hopes for her this year."

"She's so beautiful. What kind of cow is she?" Natalie asked.

"This here is a Simbrah and she's a heifer."

"A what and a what?" She was clearly out of her comfort zone. I think anyone was when speaking with Old Man Hockaday.

The old man snorted. "That's the problem with you young folk nowadays. Don't know the difference between —" he began before getting back on point. "Young lady, a heifer is a young female that has not been bred yet. And the Simbrah breed is a cross between a Simmental and a Brahma."

"Well, she certainly is a beaut," I said, not really knowing myself whether she really was a contender for breed champion or not, but I knew the ranch's reputation so I was sure my assessment of the beautiful creature was accurate.

Hockaday and I continued to chat about this year's hopefuls, while Natalie was content to stroke the heifer's head. By the time Old Man Hockaday and I had moved the topic to hunting, Natalie suddenly jumped back, reacting to the heifer's unexpected jolt to the other side of the holding pen.

"There," she pointed. "A snake. It must have spooked her."

"Damn! Looks like she twisted her leg," Hockaday said, bending over the assess the damage. The animal's leg had gotten caught in between the bars of the pen. He was able to pull her leg out, but we noticed a limp when she stepped back from the offending pen upon being freed.

"I can help," Natalie said in such a low voice I don't think the old man heard her.

I turned to look at Natalie. She wanted to try to heal the animal herself with her healing powers. I hadn't seen her use her powers since she healed my own leg, and I was curious to see if she could help the animal. I then looked over at Old Man Hockaday. "Sir, why don't you let Natalie take a look? She's really good with animals."

"I know you mean well boy, but what can she do to help?"

"Well, for starters, she's a natural around animals. You saw how Natalie was with her just now before she got spooked. Perhaps she can calm her down enough before the vet comes over. What can it hurt? The animal will either limp into the ring or limp into the ring."

He evaluated the situation and figured there wasn't much Natalie could do to hurt the animal any more than she already was. "Just watch over her while I go run and get Doc Smith. Don't let anyone get near her, ya hear?"

The second he left the stall I nodded to Natalie to do her thing. If memory served, the vet's office wasn't too far from the livestock barns, so I wanted to make sure she was able to do her thing before Hockaday returned back with the vet.

For not having spent much time around animals, Natalie really was a natural around them. She knelt gently next to the heifer and whispered something to her that sounded a lot like cooing. She then placed her hand around the heifer's right leg and pressed gently around the injury. The animal tried to jump back, probably scared by the contact, but Natalie managed to hold her steady, which was no small feat considering the animal weighed close to a thousand pounds.

In what seemed like just a minute or two, Natalie rose from her position and smiled. The heifer walked forward without a limp, her leg fully restored. I was about to tell her how impressed I was when both Old Man Hockaday and the vet ran up to the stall.

"Well, I'll be," Hockaday said.

Yeah, my sentiments exactly.

"Looks like she wasn't injured too badly after all. She was probably just shocked by all the excitement," the vet said, giving the animal another once over.

Hockaday was relieved and understandably so. To outsiders looking in, I'm sure it was hard to understand why it was so important to the old man to have his prized cattle paraded around a show ring at a small county fair, but it was actually quite simple when you came right down to it. It wasn't much different than those big dog kennel shows like Westminster or the Eukenuba Championship. Once breeders throughout the state get wind of a prize bull or heifer, it was all business.

Livestock wasn't the only thing paraded around and ranked for appearance during the show's weeklong festivities. Every year, young women between the ages of seventeen and twenty-two were encouraged to submit their applications to participate in the annual Livestock Cover Girl pageant, scheduled a week before the actual show. Every girl in the county vied for a spot on the court. The winners were presented on the first night of the show during a coronation presentation. Those lucky enough to place in the pageant presided over the show's events and were there to look pretty while passing out the awards throughout the week. To some, it was a bigger event than the actual animal judging. The only difference was, instead of spraying lacquer on a cow's tail, it was girls spritzing gallons of hairspray and applying enough make-up to make even Mary Kay Ash proud.

Natalie wanted to see what all the fuss was about, so we went over to where the contestants were being held before the crowning ceremony. It wasn't much different from the animal holding areas we'd seen earlier that day.

While the winner of the pageant, along with the other runner-ups, had already been chosen by the selection committee, the results were unknown to the contestants themselves or the general public. The coronation tonight would reveal this year's Cover Girl, who would then presume her duties for the remainder of the fair.

No one stopped us from entering the building reserved for the court. After a quick scan of the room, it didn't take long to spot Kelsey going ballistic in front of the mirror. Neither us were sure if we should approach. Curiosity got the better of us, so we headed over to her dressing station.

"What's going on Kels?" I asked.

Kelsey, facing the large mirror, turned to face us coming toward her. "Are you blind? Can't you see the ginormous zit on my chin? I can't possibly go on stage now." As an afterthought, she turned her attention to Natalie. "What? You think this is funny?"

"Not in the least," Natalie said, hiding a smile. "But perhaps I can help. I know a remedy that can reduce the size."

In spite of everything Kelsey had done to make Natalie feel unwelcome in this town, I was kinda proud to see Natalie turn the other cheek and try to help her out. I had no doubt Natalie could heal the blemish before Kelsey even got up on stage.

Kelsey snorted. "Right, like you could do anything that'll work in the next ten minutes. Do you not understand what's at stake if I'm not up there looking my best?" This was Kelsey's last year for eligibility. I wasn't around last year, but word around town was, she had competed last year and came out first runner-up. This year, she was determined to be named Mesquite County Livestock Cover Girl.

"Really, let me help," Natalie said.

"Come on Kels. What could it hurt?" It was the second time that day I pleaded with someone to take a chance on Natalie.

Kelsey looked at the two of us knowing she had no other options. "Fine. It's not like you can do anything worse to my face." She sat down in front of the mirror to allow Natalie to inspect and treat the zit. "Just don't pop it or anything. The last thing I need is a scar."

I watched silently as Natalie rooted around in her purse for something. By now, I wouldn't be too surprised if I found out she kept potions handy for emergencies.

Satisfied with what she pulled out of her bag, Natalie dipped her finger in the ointment and rubbed it gently on Kelsey's chin area. "There," she said. "It should reduce the swelling pretty fast and the committee won't be able to see a thing."

Kelsey stood up and leaned into the mirror. "How long should I keep this stuff on? It's greasy and it smells."

Natalie smiled. "It'll absorb into the skin. Just leave it alone and you'll be okay. And you're welcome."

"Whatever. Thanks. Now if you two will excuse me, I have to finishing prepping."

If Natalie expected anything more than that, she didn't let on. We walked back out onto the show grounds and went in search of food before the coronation started. I was interested to see how Natalie's treatment worked out. Frankly, I could care less if Kelsey's skin was clear or whether or not she won the pageant, but I was curious just the same.

"That was a nice thing you did back there. Do you think your healing charms worked on her face? What'd you put on that zit anyway?"

Natalie grinned. "Just good ol' fashion Carmex. You should know by now I don't need any fancy creams or ointments to heal but she doesn't have to know that."

I didn't even need confirmation on whether or not Natalie successfully healed Kelsey's nasty zit. I knew she did. "You know your secret's safe with me. Although I must say I'm impressed at how you handled Hockaday's heifer earlier today. You should apply to be the show's vet next year."

"Well, heifers are my speciality," she laughed along with me. The dig on Kelsey wasn't lost on me.

We didn't want to go to the coronation, so we spent the rest of the afternoon enjoying the fair and I even one her one of those damned stuffed animals at the carnival later that night. After I saw how she handled Old Hockaday's heifer, and even Kelsey, I began to admire the awesome responsibility Natalie had as a Healer. I could also see why someone like her sister would try to abuse that power.

Sixteen

The next day, I thought I'd surprise Natalie with an evening alone. We had fun at the livestock show, but I had something more intimate in mind. It wasn't one of the more romantic dates I'd ever planned, but in my experience, planning too much in advance was overrated anyway—nothing every played out according to plan. Before leaving the house, I'd packed a cooler and made sure I had plenty of CD's to play before we headed out to the river. I was hoping to make tonight special, as a way of apologizing for the ass I'd been the last couple of days.

I still couldn't get a handle on everything and why she seemed to suffer from short-term memory loss—we never did get around to discussing that—but I was content to shelve the matter for awhile. I could wait and let me into her world in her own time. The God's honest truth was, I just didn't want to talk about it.

We laid on a blanket in the bed of my pick-up as we gazed up at the full moon. George Strait crooned in the background about love, ocean front property, and a multitude of ex's, while the comfortable silence between us created its own melodic harmony.

Natalie was definitely unlike any other girl I'd gone out with. Back at Tulane, I had the unfortunate pleasure of entertaining several girls that were just as self-centered and entitled as Kelsey was back in high school. It was as if I were a magnet that only attracted the gilded lilies, only to discover the trash buried beneath the surface. But this wasn't the case with Natalie. She actually seemed pleased with our date so far and didn't seem to care that I took her to the river in my beat-up old Ford with just a cooler of beer (Shiner, of course) and outdated country music.

Lying down on the scratchy plaid blanket, I turned my head to look at her. I realized again for the second time that—for she was almost as tall as I—our mouths matched up almost perfectly; our bodies almost proportionate in length. I had the reoccurring thought of what it would it would be like to kiss her again. I decided I was tired of wondering and didn't bother to ask whether or not it was okay.

It turned out I didn't have to ask. Like a magnetized force, our mouths found each other and every feeling I'd ever had when being with a girl was distant memory compared to what I felt at that moment. The kiss was every bit as intense as that night she kissed me after dancing at Caldero's.

From the very first time I met her, she always appeared distant and reserved, but now, lying with me on the back of the truck, she was uninhibited and welcomed my roaming hands and lips. She herself felt comfortable exploring my body and I knew we were about to reach that moment there was no turning back. Then, as if what we were about to do finally dawned on her, she pushed me aside.

"Wyatt, we have to stop," she said, pulling down her shirt that had ridden up while we made out like a couple of horny teenagers on the musty old blanket. "I can't."

"Why not?" Not two seconds ago, I felt like we were finally in sync with each other. Hell, her own body language was telling me something different than her words—she wanted me as much as I wanted her.

"I just can't. I want to, trust me, I do, but now's not the right time."

"Is there ever?" It came out more like a mumble, as I wasn't really surprised by the turn of events. This was just par for the course with Natalie. She always had a secret, or something she didn't want to discuss and then just clammed up. I had just hoped that this time, she'd be more willing to be more open with me, and not just in a sexual way. I thought that if I gave her some space, she would be more forthcoming. "Is it me? Did I do something wrong? It's not your first time is it?" Maybe that was it. I had pressured her into doing something she wasn't ready for.

She managed a small smile. "Actually, yeah, but that's not why we have stop."

Her admission kind of surprised me, but I also I knew this didn't have anything to do with modesty or integrity. What was happening between us was more than just lust, there was more to it than just getting laid, and I knew she wanted me as much as I wanted her. Call me crazy, but with everything she'd been hiding—with good reason—I figured there was another piece of the puzzle she wasn't willing to part with, which had nothing to do with protecting her virtue.

"Look, if I'm being out of line, just say so, but if it has to do with well, you know, being some kind of higher power, you can tell me that, too."

For a second I was afraid she wasn't going to say anything at all, but she finally looked up at me and began to explain. "It's my sister."

For the second time in one night she was able to throw me yet another curveball—more so than the fact that she was still a virgin. This was an explanation I had not been expecting. "What does this have to do with your sister?" Hell, I didn't even know she *had* a sister.

"She's here," she said, as if it answered everything.

Again, this seemed to come out of left field. What did this have to do with us being together? "What do you mean she's here? Is she here for a visit or something?" Every time I thought I had a handle on the situation, she threw something else out there for me to figure out.

"No, nothing like that. It's worse. See, she's like me, only she's bad. Really bad."

"What do you mean?" By now, I had almost forgotten what got us to this point in the conversation, as I was confused by what she was telling me. I'd long forgotten about feeling her pressed up against my body, kissing her soft lips, being that close to her.

"I'm not always comfortable with my gifts. That's where the choice part of the equation comes into play. I don't have to use my powers at all if I choose not to. But it was kind of expected so I can carry on the family tradition of healers. Portia on the other hand relished in her powers and for the wrong reasons. She never wanted any part of being a healer like the rest of us. In her mind, since they already had me to accept their tradition, she was free to do as she pleased. So she sought out other ways to use her power. And not in a good way."

"So you guys can do other things aside from healing?"

"We weren't born with the instincts to use our gifts for anything other than to heal, but because we have powers, we can pretty much do anything. I mean, we're not powerful enough to conjure things out of thin air, but close enough."

"Okay, so what does that have to do with your sister?"

"When she realized there weren't limits to what she could do, she went out and looked for ways to become more powerful. And she did. Every ounce of knowledge she consumed only made her that much more dangerous. To the point she became an unstoppable force. That's one of the reasons my parents sent me here to stay with my *tías*."

"To keep you safe," I finished for her, assuming I was hearing her correctly. "And now she's here."

She nodded. "But I'm also here to continue my teaching."

"But you said—"

"Just because I was born with these gifts doesn't mean they come with an instruction manual. Way back when, before we became hybrid type beings, The Ancient Ones were born with the intrinsic knowledge to heal. That was what separated them from regular shamans or witch doctors. Once they began to mix with humans, that knowledge got blurred. The human hybrids were born with the power, but without the instincts. My aunts have been designated to serve as my guides so I learn the ways of healing, yet at the same time learn how to control my powers. Just like anything else in this world, absolute power corrupts absolutely. Other born Healers, like my sister, have taken on more than they were meant to handle.

"With the proper tutelage and guidance, beings with my abilities can use their power for good, but there are others that try to absorb too much. It's like a drug. If you take on too much, there's no coming back from that. My sister Portia didn't want to listen and continued to seek more magic for herself from anyone that would give it to her."

"Why would she want to do that?"

"Like I said before, power. With everything she's attained, she can became pretty damn unstoppable. She can be, and probably already is, just as powerful, if not more, than any other Healer."

"And your aunts? How do they fit into the picture aside from guiding you? Why didn't they take Portia under their wing like you?"

"I was sent here initially for them watch over and protect me. All of this came after we realized Portia's true motives. Normally, I would have just stayed with my parents to learn, but when Portia got out of control, my aunts intervened."

It sounded weird to hear one needed protecting from their own sibling. "What happened with your sister to make her like that?"

"As the youngest, Portia never liked being, in her opinion, second best. She always enjoyed being the center of attention. My parents tried so hard to teach her the rules of being a Healer, but she resisted it at every turn."

"So she went in search of more power for herself," I finished for her. It was an easy assumption.

Natalie nodded. "You have to understand, when my sister wants something, she doesn't hold back. She sought the greatest source of black magic she could find. It's the only kind that would allow her to absorb more than she was born to consume."

"Why do you keep referring to her in the past tense?"

"Portia became very powerful, very quickly. When the Great Priests figured out what my sister was up to, they condemned her to a life within the body of a special host to contain all that power. It was the only way to control her without killing her."

"What do you mean they trapped her in a body? You said she was here in town."

"No. I said she was here. Enclosed in a corporeal vessel to suppress all that power inside her. Trapped."

I knew what was coming, but I still had to ask. "Whose body?"

"Mine."

My first instinct was to run. Again. Just jump off from the back of the pick-up and drive away. Her sister was trapped in her body? "What the fuck, Natalie? I was willing to overlook the whole healing thing because I've actually witnessed it with my own eyes and I can't ignore that, but this?"

"I know how ridiculous this all sounds. Trust me, I do. Sometimes I find it hard to believe myself," she said.

I calmed down long enough to hear her out. "When did all this happen? When they put her in you, I mean." I knew she wasn't lying about being a Healer, and I couldn't argue with what I've already seen, so I decided to listen to what she had to say.

She sighed, not sure if she should go on. "It wasn't easy locating her at first, but once the Great Priests did, they locked her up inside me. That was about two years ago. She'd pretty much been dormant all this time, but now she's figured out a way to use her magic to break free from time to time.

"I wasn't ever planning on telling you about what I am, but when you started talking about my memory lapses, I decided to tell you about being a Healer, and when you freaked about that, I thought I'd keep the part about my sister myself."

"I can understand why you'd feel that way." I was trying to keep an open mind.

"Do you? Do you really? Because if you don't, that's fine. That's why I didn't want to get involved, but you never stopped trying. If you want to bail, this is your out."

Did she expect me to decide this instant? "I just don't know what to say. I mean, you can't just tell me something like this and expect me to just believe it. I need some time."

"It's okay, I understand. I don't blame you if you don't want to have anything to do with me."

Was I really going to consider what she just told me? Now that I've finally broken down that wall of hers, was I ready to give up on her? No, I decided I believed her. If she was able to heal me, then she was probably telling me the truth about this, too. "Look, let's say I believe you. What then? I want to be with you and now you're telling me you can't because you have another being inside you."

"Now do you understand why it's hard to be around you? I can't bear the thought of my sister taking over when I'm with you. And from what's been going on these last few days, I know now that she's been successful."

It all came together then, like a jigsaw puzzle that doesn't begin to form a picture until it was a third of the way complete. Natalie's insistence on keeping her distance from me. The memory lapses. The erratic and irresponsible behavior. Now I knew why she had tried so hard to keep me away from her. It was like having a split personality.

And I couldn't ignore the fact that I already had the pleasure of meeting Portia. That Sunday at Hector's when

Natalie showed up looking like one of those tacky flamingo lawn ornaments. And at Tyler's party. "Now I know why you freaked when I told you about Hector's that Sunday I went over for dinner."

"When you told me I was there I didn't know what to think. I knew it was her, but I couldn't believe she had the nerve to seek you out. That's why I wanted you to leave and forget about me."

I pulled her closer to me. "Well, I hope you know that's not going to happen."

"I know it's not a promise you can keep, but I'll take it for now."

"Don't say that. It's going to be okay," I whispered in her ear. "She's not here now. Only us."

"No, but that doesn't mean she can't stop by for a visit."

We sat that way for a while. Only this time, the silence between us was more like a chord out of tune than a harmony in sync.

I was the first to speak up. "So, about us..."

She knew what I meant. Maybe we were in sync after all. "Sex isn't even an option. Not with my sister, well, you know," she said.

It never occurred to me just how much Natalie was giving up because of what she was.

"You don't have to look so pathetic about it. I've come to terms with it, ya know?"

"It just doesn't seem fair."

"Life isn't fair."

"I guess not," I said, thinking about my own warped family life. "So how does it work? Can she just appear whenever she wants?" I shuddered at the thought. If I were to ever get involved with Natalie—which now seemed like an impossibility—I didn't know if I could handle the idea of her sister taking over her body in intimate situations.

"She doesn't have the strength to take over indefinitely, I don't think, for something like that, but the threat is always there."

"How exactly is she able to take over, anyway? I'm guessing it can't be that easy."

"She tends to come through when my defenses are down. Like when I'm sleeping, tired, stressed, whatever. Not all the time, but those seem to be prime windows of opportunity for her. Every time she appears, it takes a lot out of her, so she can only take over for short periods of time."

The idea that her sister could take over her body bothered me to the point of developing goose bumps along my arms. If we were ever to get intimate and Portia came through, I couldn't imagine what that would do to Natalie, not to mention me. "So if you and I were to, you know, she could use that to her advantage?" Again, I shuddered at the thought.

"Well, I haven't exactly tested out that theory, but I would imagine if I let my guard down, yes, she could very well take over."

"Okay, so this is really a dumb question, given the direction this conversation has taken, but how did they manage to trap an entire being inside you?"

It was a legitimate question, but Natalie ended up bursting out laughing at my expense. "She's not literally inside me. Her physical form is being held in some undisclosed location and they won't even tell *me* where she is."

"Then—"

"It's her *soul* that resides within me."

In a weird way, that made sense. "So basically what you're telling me is that they've turned you into Bruce Banner. Or Dr. Jekyll."

"I get Dr. Jekyll, but who's Bruce Banner?"

"You don't know The Hulk? He's Bruce Banner's alter ego."

"Ah, gotcha. Yeah, the Hulk always comes out when confronted or during high levels of stress."

"Exactly." Which really didn't sound so cool once you actually said it out loud. "So, how long does she have to be trapped inside you?"

Natalie looked at me with a grave expression on her face. "Forever. Or until they can figure out a way to expel her and contain her powers. They can't risk having her expose her powers. But that's not likely to happen, I'm afraid."

"Hold up, who's they?" I was so caught up in her story I missed something.

"Like I said earlier. The Great Priests. The priests that locked her away. The ones that have been assigned to protect our secrets."

"You mean like regular priests?" I had a hard time picturing Father Hilario over at St. Cecilia's being a part of a grand conspiracy like this. I wondered if Carmen knew anything about the Great Priests and the secrets they kept. If she did, it would explain why she spent a lot of time in church.

"Yes and no. The Great Priests are real priests in the conventional sense, but a selected few are chosen the Keepers of the Watch. Every parish has one that protects our secrets and watches for any potential threat to our kind. They are a great source of knowledge and guidance."

"I'll bet." I was an equal opportunity skeptic. I had my doubts about any organized religion just as much as the legends and myths they were based on. And as a result, I had stopped going to church years ago. I can't say that I'd given up on faith, I just preferred to believe in my own way.

"What do you have against priests?"

"Nothing really, I just don't buy into the dogma."

"You don't believe in anything do you?" Only it came out more like a statement than a question.

I had to tread very carefully in how I chose to respond. If I was too quick to deny any form of religious belief, Natalie could take it the wrong way thinking I didn't believe all that she had told me thus far. "I'm open to a lot of things, I guess. I just prefer not to put all my eggs in one basket."

"Fair enough."

Seventeen

I was a mess on the inside—flux of emotions ran through me ranging from furious to confused. All I wanted to do was hop in my truck and drive back to New Orleans. It wasn't fair to Natalie, and I was the last to admit it, but she was right. Her problems were complex and complicated. I wanted to run away not only from my problems, like I had four years ago, but from hers too. There was nothing keeping me here. My mother was out of touch with reality, I got in Carmen's way, and now with Natalie and her problems, it was easier to just pack my bags and go.

But something held me back. Something deep inside told me leaving Natalie would be a mistake. All I needed was some time to reflect on everything that had happened. It'd been two days since I last reached out to her and I felt like a jerk, but I needed some time to digest everything. I wasn't trying to purposely avoid her again, but I did need to get a handle over my emotions, so I headed over to Tyler's house, hoping he could get my mind off everything that had happened over the last week. He could talk about football 'till the cows came home. I didn't care, I just needed a distraction to take my mind off Natalie for a while.

His folks didn't live too far from me, so I didn't have a real chance to be alone with my thoughts by the time I got to his house. I knew his parents were at work, so I just let myself in as I always had since childhood. "Hey, Ty," I called out from the doorway.

"We're in here," I heard Tyler calling out from the living room.

If I wanted to take my mind of Natalie, coming here wasn't going to accomplish that. I walked into the room and in that instant I felt like I had been punched in the gut. The last thing I expected was to see Natalie sitting on the couch with Tyler. Cozied up would be a more appropriate assessment. Tyler knew I had something going on with Natalie and yet there they were, snuggled together as if I were of no concern.

"What the hell?" I was fuming on the inside.

"Hi, Wyatt," Natalie said, not bothering to move away from Tyler on the couch. "Tyler and I were just getting to know each other a little better."

Just from the inflection in her voice, I knew instantly that it wasn't Natalie but Portia. How could I have forgotten so quickly after what Natalie confided in me? Another dead giveaway was her outfit—Natalie/Portia was outfitted once again in bright pink from head to toe. The classic shift dress reminded me of a 1950's housewife. In the few run-ins I've had with Portia, she always seemed favor bright preppy get-ups, as opposed to Natalie's penchant for cutoffs and t-shirts.

For a brief moment, I felt a surge of relief that it was Portia and not Natalie. But the relief I felt was short-lived —Tyler didn't know it wasn't Natalie. Yet there they were on his couch. This wasn't exactly a good situation either way. Portia was out of her corporeal prison and who knew what she's been doing with my best friend. I had to get Natalie/Portia out of his house without alerting him.

"Aw, what's with all the grump, Grumpy McGrumperson? Don't you wanna join the party?" Portia was taunting me. Her tone made me rethink whether or not she knew I was on to her. "Tyler here has beer."

"Yeah, Wyatt. You're welcome to hang out," Tyler said, knowing full well I was pissed about seeing Natalie/Portia in his home. But he did his best to play it off like it was nothing. For his own set of reasons, I guess he didn't want to cause a scene either.

"Natalie, I think you better go." The best course of action was to play like I was jealous. Although Natalie never actually came out and said so, something told me that Portia couldn't possibly know I was aware of her existence. I had my doubts after the way she was carrying on now, but if I played along, pretending to be speaking with Natalie, it would be my best defense against Portia. At the very least for Tyler's sake. No need to get him involved.

"Why? I just got here," she with a pout. I was very familiar with that look. It was the same one Kelsey loved to give—it was the look of defiance, a challenge of sorts. "Tyler and I were having a good time. Weren't we?"

"Dude, relax. She just came over to say hi," Tyler stepped in to defend Natalie/Portia. "We were actually talking about you."

"You and I have a few things we need to discuss," I said, ignoring his excuses. I looked at Portia square in the eye. "I'm sure you don't mind if Ty and I have a little chat do you?"

She pretended to think about it for a moment before bouncing off the couch. "Sure," she said. "I'll be seeing y'all around."

I waited until she went outside, presumably on her way home, or wherever she decided to strike next, before talking to Tyler. I only hoped that Portia wouldn't get herself into trouble while using Natalie's body. Knowing Portia was out and about around town, I probably should have kept an eye on her instead, but I had to get her away from Tyler to protect both Natalie from whatever was about to happen before I stopped by, and my best friend from making a big error in judgment.

He also waited for her to leave the house before reading me the riot act. "What the hell was that about? We were just hanging out. I wasn't going to make a play for her, I swear. She just stopped by to ask about you. Really."

"You're seriously asking me that? You were alone with Natalie," I accused. I knew he'd never intentionally jeopardize our friendship over a girl, and I knew it really wasn't Natalie, but I was still pissed off at having seen him with her.

His face softened. "You know I'd never steal a chick you were interested in on purpose. But what I don't understand is why you're getting all worked up over a girl. She's totally hot, I'll give you that, but it's not like you're sticking around."

"It's not that. She's special." This time I was being honest, at least in part. I really did have feelings for her and if Portia hadn't been the reason for me to flip out, I would've still been just as upset seeing Natalie here. If only I was able to tell him the whole truth.

Tyler continued to study me. "I think there's something else going on that you're not telling me. I know you like her and all, and you know I'd never make a move, no matter how irresistible I am to chicks," he said, in an attempt to lighten the tension between us. "And for the record, she was the one making the moves."

I almost laughed. Tyler could take what could have been an uncomfortable situation, no matter how one sided it was, and make it okay. I wasn't entirely surprised to find out Portia was hitting on Tyler. "Like I said, she's special, that's all."

"Dude, you know you can tell me anything and I know something must be up. You wouldn't be actin' this way if there weren't."

"Look man, I know you wouldn't do anything to jeopardize our friendship, especially over a girl, but I can't really go into it now."

He shrugged, as if to say, "no skin off my back," before actually saying, "All I know is, I hope you know what you're doing with that chick. Like I said, she was seriously putting the moves on me and I know how much you're into her. Just be careful."

How do I explain to Tyler it wasn't Natalie who stopped by for a visit, but her evil sister that was forever cast into her body and could appear without a moment's notice? I couldn't. Even if I believed it, I didn't know if I could even say it with a straight face. I was afraid that if I said it out loud, I'd see the absurdity of it all—through Tyler's eyes.

"Trust me, I know what I'm doing and I wish I could explain, but it's kind of complicated." God, I was even starting to sound like Natalie. I wondered how long I would be able to go through this charade. Until all hell broke loose? Until I went back home to New Orleans?

Tyler shrugged it off. "Sure. And whatever it is, it can't be all that bad, right? You barely even know the girl."

Leave it to Ty to bring some added perspective into the matter. In a way, he was right. Perhaps I shouldn't get all worked up over a girl I barely even know, but somehow, ignoring all that had happened didn't sit right with me, either. I was already in too deep.

Eighteen

When I thought enough time had passed, knowing Portia couldn't control Natalie's body long, I headed over to her house. I wanted to check up on Natalie and see if she was okay. My first instinct was to head straight over to her house after leaving Tyler's, but I didn't want to freak Natalie out by making a fuss all over her. Besides, she probably needed some time to recoup. I'm sure having a foreign spirit take over your body had to be tiresome. So an hour after I left Tyler's house, and after reassuring him that everything was fine—not to mention reassuring myself—I jumped into my truck and headed for the fading, grand Queen Anne Victorian, hoping Portia had gone back into the prison cell that was Natalie.

It took forever for Natalie to answer the door, which caused me to worry even more. What if Portia was still out? Just as I was ready to do a little breaking and entering, Natalie finally appeared at the door. As soon as the door creaked open, she collapsed into my arms. "It happened again, didn't it?" she asked.

She looked so exhausted and frail, all I wanted to do was continue to hold her in my arms and protect her forever. For some reason, I expected Natalie to have a full recollection of her sister's exploits. "Don't you remember anything at all?"

"Not much. I was about to head over to the restaurant to help with lunch service and the next thing I knew, I was in my room."

"So you don't remember going over to Tyler's house today?"

Natalie's face went pale. "No. What was I doing there?"

I knew what she was asking. "Don't worry, nothing happened. I went over there to clear my head and you were already there. Apparently, you went over to pump Ty for information about me," I assured her. There was no need to upset her by telling her what Tyler said about Portia making advances. "At least, that's what I think she was doing there. She was cozied up with him, but nothing worth worrying about."

"That must have been tough for you, seeing me there," she said.

I just shrugged and offered her a smile, not wanting to make a bigger deal out of it than it already was, especially since she seemed shaken up by the whole incident. "It's okay, I made you go home. I'm not really sure if your sister knew I was aware of her or not, but she left when I asked her to. I wasn't sure what else to do."

"No, you did the right thing. I'm not exactly sure what she's capable of doing when she takes over. My sister has an overactive libido when she's around guys, especially hot ones, so I'm glad you arrived when you did."

"So you think Ty's hot, huh?" I joked. "Should I be concerned?"

She laughed, finally calming down since hearing about today's incident involving Portia. "You know what I mean."

I hugged her again. "We'll figure this out, okay" I said. "Can't we?"

"I don't think we can. Until the Great Priests can find a way to contain her without using me as a vessel, I'm stuck with her."

"But they're looking for a way, right?" I waited and didn't get an immediate response. "Right?" I asked again.

Natalie just looked saddened. "I told you it was forever. I'm pretty much resigned to the fact that they won't find a way to help me."

"Why?" How could these priests resign themselves to hurting Natalie?

"Because if Portia ever got back out into the world she'd wreak enough havoc to draw attention to our powers. Everything the Great Priests have been bound to protect will be exposed."

"So they don't want to help."

"That's what I think."

"What happens now?"

"Nothing. I'm afraid that in time, she'll figure out a way to take over my body permanently. Even though she's contained in me, she still has access to our power. If she were ever able to control me completely, all she has to do is tap into mine."

That part never occurred to me. It was a scary thought, knowing Portia had the ability to use Natalie's power. "There's got to be a way. I won't let up until we figure it out, okay?"

"To what end, Wyatt? I mean, you're only here for what, a few more weeks? And then what?"

I stood there momentarily stunned. "You actually think after all this, I'm just going to run out and leave you? After everything I told you about my dad and leaving us, do you really think I'd just abandon you like that?"

"What am I supposed to think? You've never said anything about sticking around. And I don't expect you to. You're about to start medical school, or did you forget? This isn't your problem, Wyatt. Once you're gone, I'm back to dealing with this on my own."

I couldn't believe she had such a low opinion of me. "God, Natalie. Do you think I'm that much of an asshole? Aren't I the one that just rescued you from what could have been a compromising situation over at Tyler's? Even if I were to ditch you, wouldn't it still be good to find a way to get rid of that force that's inside you?"

She wasn't convinced. "I promised myself a long time ago that I wouldn't get attached to anyone. And now that I have, I realized that it was all for good reason. This," she pointed her finger, indicating the two of us, "was exactly what I was afraid would happen if I did."

"I'm not leaving you, Natalie." No sooner did the words leave my mouth, I knew it was the truth.

I must have made her uncomfortable, because she looked away from me. "Look, let's take this conversation upstairs."

"Upstairs?" For a moment, it felt like high school all over again—awed that a girl would invite me up to her room. It felt so taboo, so deliciously exciting. I must not have freaked her out by my admission if she was asking me to go upstairs with her.

"I just don't want my aunts to come home and find us talking about this. If you haven't already figured out, they can be nosy when it comes to me and my relationships."

I followed her up the staircase. "What's up with that, anyway? I would think that because of what you are and what's going on with your sister, they'd want to keep you under lock and key."

She seemed disheartened by the question I posed. "You know, I've thought about that too, and I've come to the conclusion that they want me to experience a bit of life before it's too late. They can't offer me any more than that."

Before it's too late. Which by that theory meant that her aunts had lost all hope for her. Hearing this saddened me. It was like a Make-a-Wish goodwill gesture for demonically possessed victims—*Make-A-Friend before your sister devours your spirit.* I decided then and there I would find a way to change all that. If there was ever a determining factor—a defining moment—this was it. I would find a way to make Natalie whole again.

Nineteen

Conflicting thoughts ran through my head. Everything I believed to be true about the human body and how it functioned on a molecular level was wrong according to what I now knew of the Healers. After seeing what Natalie could do, there had to be countless other possibilities that were beyond the scope of even modern day science. Maybe Arthur C. Clarke was on to something when he came up with the three laws of prediction. In one, he states that you have to venture into the impossible to discover the limits of the possible. Perhaps science and magic really are interchangeable. Well, that's one theory, anyway.

I needed more answers and there was one person I was close enough to ask. Carmen. I hadn't visited Carmen in her bedroom ever since that time I stumbled upon her tarot cards, but she was the best resource I had and fortunately for me, we shared the same roof.

The door to her bedroom was closed, which was normal. As a member of the family, she required a certain amount of privacy, and we respected that. I rapped my knuckles lightly against the door's wooden frame and waited for Carmen to open the door. I half hoped she wouldn't hear me knocking, giving me a way out of having this conversation altogether, but she heard it and answered her door.

"*Mijito*, what's wrong?" Carmen asked. Worry filled her voice. In all the years she'd cared for me, I had never come to her room unannounced unless I was ill and needed attention. This was of course after my own mother couldn't be bothered to take care of me herself. She'd left that responsibility, along with everything else, to Carmen.

"Nothing serious. I just want to talk," I assured her, motioning for her to open the door to let me in.

Reluctantly, she gave in and patted the bed for me to sit. It had been years since I'd set foot in her room and from I remember, nothing had changed. I glanced around the small room she had called home for over forty years. For all intents and purposes, this house was run and belonged to Carmen. She was the true mistress of the house. With my mother out of commission for almost half of the years that Carmen had been in her employ, she was the one that deserved the grand master bedroom upstairs, not the small bedroom located on the first floor next to the kitchen.

It was a small room, aside from a modest crucifix affixed above her door; the walls were bare with the exception of a few photos of her family in Mexico taped to her mirror, a portrait of Jesus, and of course, a framed photo of new Latin American *papa*, Pope Francis. She had a small television set on one of the side tables—tuned in to one of her *telenovelas*. On her dresser was an elaborate box made to resemble some kind of altar, complete with brightly colored trinkets and more photos.

"*Es un niche*," she said, noting my interest in the little altar.

"A niche?"

"For my *ofrendas*."

"*Ofrendas*." I thought for a moment. "Offerings?"

"*Sí*. Offerings…gifts," she explained.

I nodded in understanding. "That's what I wanted to talk to you about," I said, taking a deep breath before speaking again. "What can you tell me about the magic you do?"

"¿Por qué? *La magia* is no something you need to know," she said. To her credit, she didn't appear upset or even surprised by my questions as I originally thought she'd be—like the last time I ventured into her room to snoop. It was as if she knew I'd come around asking at some point and was just waiting for the day I'd come once again to ask questions.

"I was just wondering. You never talk about it, you don't want me to know about it, yet you always conduct business here at the house. I guess I was just curious."

She nodded in understanding. "Natalia. You ask because of her."

"Yes. I want to know more about her and what y'all are mixed up in." I didn't mean for it to come out confrontational, but it did. I was so sure Carmen would have the answers and I wasn't leaving until she gave me something.

"You need to stay away, *mijito*. She no good for you," she said.

I was hoping to get some answers, but not this. "How can you say that? She's Amelia and Ester's niece. Aren't they your friends?"

"*Sí, pero* she no good for you," she said again. "It better you leave her alone."

I couldn't believe I was hearing this, especially coming from Carmen. "The sisters obviously have a different opinion on the matter. They've never treated me like anything other than family, yet you're telling to stay away from their niece? What's really going on? Why are you telling me this now?"

Carmen refused to meet my eyes. "Now you start asking questions."

This was absurd. I had hoped Carmen would find my interest as a sign that I was willing to accept everything I had come to learn about magic and her vocation. It seemed now that the more I knew and questioned it, the more she refused to discuss the matter. For years, she had a knack for meddling in my business, but when it came down to her own, she closed herself off. In a way, it was more hurtful than my mother shutting me out—Carmen was conscious of what she was doing.

"Please Carmen, tell me about the magic. About the Healers."

"*No*. I made a *promesa* to your mother."

"What does she have to do with it? The woman doesn't even remember what day of the week it is." I wondered just how much my mother actually knew about Carmen and her dealings in Mexican folk healing. Having spent most of her life around Carmen, I bet there was a time when my mother knew more than she was able to remember these days.

"*No*." She was adamant this time. "I cannot."

The *telenovela* was still playing in the background. There was a lot of yelling and someone on the show was being pushed down the stairs. I didn't understand most of what they were saying, the actors were speaking so fast, but I got the gist. It's exactly how I felt after having this conversation with Carmen—like someone was trying to get me out of the way.

Twenty

Things were slowly going back into what I considered a normal routine, if you could consider anything about my relationship with Natalie normal. As far as we knew, Portia hadn't made an appearance in a few weeks and Natalie was finally giving us a chance to get to know each other better. Aside from serving breakfast and supper, Carmen had been avoiding me, but I imagine she was afraid I'd start asking questions again.

It seemed like everyone was in good spirits at The Pit one late Friday night in August. Football season was almost upon the town and the high school football varsity team was already showing up for early morning trainings and playing scrimmages with some of the other local teams. Tonight they played against the Tigers and our team was a tour de force, creaming them 21-3. Everyone had stopped by after the scrimmage, and the conversation around the restaurant was alive, rehashing every play-by-play. According to the chatter around the restaurant, tonight's game was considered a good predictor for the rest of the season.

Natalie and I missed the game, but we stopped by The Pit to celebrate with the rest of the town. Texas high school football ruled and we wanted to support our local team, even if we couldn't make the scrimmage.

It was so crowded, we were seated smack in the center of the restaurant, so we weren't afforded the privacy we usually enjoyed when we took over one of the corner booths. I left Natalie alone for a moment to place our order. On busy nights, you actually had to go up to the counter and tell them what you wanted.

On my way back to our table, I could overhear Kelsey say, "Did you guys know that Natalie reads tarot cards? I totally think she should read our fortunes. What do you think?"

I knew then that nothing good was to come of Kelsey's idea. Only I didn't know if it would end badly on her end or Natalie's. I knew her suggestion wasn't going to go well either way.

"I don't think that's a very good idea," Natalie said, shaking her head. "Besides, no one really wants to hear their futures told."

"Oh come on, don't spoil the fun. You have the cards on you, don't you? I always see you carrying them around in your pocket. We're bored anyway, so you might as well keep us entertained," Kelsey insisted.

I knew Kelsey was only doing this to make Natalie look like a joke. Fortunately, the others that had centered around the table were thinking anything but. Tyler was sitting on the opposite Kelsey in the booth, and I could tell his interest was piqued, as well as some of the others that were close enough to overhear the conversation. "That's so cool. Can I go first?" he asked.

"I guess so," Natalie said, hesitating slightly. Even though I knew the others would think it harmless, I could only imagine how she felt about displaying her talents in front of everyone. I just hoped they wouldn't tease her about it.

Kelsey moved from the other side of the table to allow Natalie to sit across from Tyler.

"Awesome. So what do I have to do?" Tyler asked.

By now, Natalie had already whipped out her cards. "Nothing, except cut the deck."

He did as instructed and we all watched as she flipped the cards that showed Tyler his past, present, and future. She made a big show of placing the cards in a triangle for Tyler's benefit.

She explained how the reading worked before asking, "You ready?"

"Go for it," Tyler said, totally engrossed by what Natalie was saying.

Natalie flipped the top card. "Ah, the Queen of Cups! You are very passionate and romantic. This tells me you have reached a higher emotional level of maturity when it comes to your relationships."

At that, I burst out laughing. "Ty, emotionally mature?"

Tyler found it just as amusing. "Dude, what can I say? I'm a master when it comes to relationships," he said, winking at Natalie.

"Yeah, a master at breaking hearts," I reminded him.

He ignored me and looked back at Natalie. "So what else?"

She flipped another card, this one his present. "The Five of Wands. This symbolizes competition and good sportsmanship. You have a great understanding and appreciation for teamwork."

"Whoa," Tyler exclaimed. "That's totally how I feel about football."

"Are you not like totally conceited?" Kelsey said, peering over his shoulder, looking at the cards.

"Get over yourself Kelsey, this is good stuff. Keep going Natalie," he urged.

"Okay, so here's your future card." She paused before turning it over. "Are you sure you want to know?" she asked.

"Totally."

For some reason, I was just as anxious as Tyler was to hear his future—we all were.

"Wow, the Ten of Coins!" Natalie looked at Tyler in astonishment.

"What? What does that mean?" Tyler didn't know whether it was good or bad.

"You'll have great wealth and security in your future," she said.

"I knew it! I'm totally going to be drafted for the NFL." Tyler was totally buying the reading and I didn't discourage him. If he wanted to believe, I wasn't going to burst his bubble.

"Oh come on guys, none of this is actually real," Kelsey said. By now, the entire restaurant was fixated on Natalie and her fortune telling. Kelsey was beginning to realize that her plan had backfired.

"It was your idea, Kels," I reminded her. "If you think it's all fake, why don't you let Natalie read *your* fortune?"

I could tell she didn't want to look like a fool for suggesting Natalie read cards, then back out by not wanting her own cards read. "Sure, I'll play along."

Everyone around the booth got quiet. While I had a feeling everyone pretty much felt the same way as Kelsey and didn't believe in having your fortune read, they were all interested to hear what Kelsey's future held. And even thought they would never admit it, I was pretty sure they were hoping it would be a misfortunate one.

We weren't disappointed.

After Natalie had Kelsey cut the deck, she laid out the cards, just as she had during Tyler's reading. Quickly, she flipped the first card. "The Ace of Swords," she announced. "See how it's upside down? There's a lot of anger buried inside you, as well as a misplaced aggressive nature."

"Bullshit," Kelsey started, but stopped short, probably realizing she was only confirming what Natalie was saying.

"Shall I continue?" Natalie asked.

Kelsey waved her hand over the cards, prompting Natalie to continue. Natalie turned over the next card. "This one is your present, represented by the Knights of Swords. Normally, this symbolizes courage, patience, and confidence in attaining one's goals, but since it's upside down, it signifies your ability to be stubborn, with a propensity to commit violence to get what you want."

This time, Kelsey restrained herself from doing or saying anything. Everyone, including Kelsey, knew that this was a pretty accurate depiction, so she kept her mouth shut.

Natalie continued with the last card. "And finally, your future. Oh," she said, stopping for dramatic effect. "The Moon."

"Let me guess, another shit card," Kelsey said, careful to control her temper.

"Not necessarily. Do you want me to continue or not?" Natalie pressed.

"Sure, go on. Please enlighten us. Tell us what the moon means," Kelsey said sarcastically.

"The Moon is actually a great card. It symbolizes one who is in touch with their dreams as well as the unknown. An ability to accept things that are beyond their scope. Basically, it means you're able to follow and achieve your dreams, even if it's farfetched."

"But it's reversed," I couldn't help but point out.

Natalie looked up from the card and smiled. "Thanks, Wyatt. Yes, when the Moon card is reversed it means the opposite, I'm afraid." She turned to look at Kelsey. "You lack the ability to follow through with your instincts and dreams. Because of that you could end up having a nervous, emotional breakdown, or become an alcoholic."

Kelsey didn't say a word at first, embarrassed that she had fallen into her own trap. She should have known the outcome of the tarot reading wasn't going to be favorable after the way she insisted on treating Natalie. Then again, maybe there was some truth behind Kelsey's fortune and it really was just all in the cards for her. Either way, I wasn't too surprised.

"See," Kelsey finally said, after taking a moment to compose herself. "I told you it was all bullshit."

"Ah, come on Kels, where's your sense of humor?" Tyler said.

"Didn't sound funny to me," Kelsey snapped back. "And of course you'd jump to her defense, you came out smelling like roses. She purposely gave me that fake fortune just to be a bitch."

Natalie just smiled. "I simply told you what the cards said. You could look up the meanings if you'd like."

That put an end to the tarot portion of the evening, and Natalie and I retreated back to our table, allowing Kelsey cool her heels before she said or did something she'd regret later. It didn't stop Kelsey from shooting daggers at Natalie the rest of the night, but at least she was far enough away not to start another confrontation.

Our food was ready by the time we got back to our table, and we were finally able to enjoy our meal when the whispers started. What had started out as community cohesiveness rallying around their hometown football victory, quickly turned into pointing fingers and whispered accusations, especially after Natalie's tarot demonstration. Kelsey used that to her advantage by pointing out Natalie's differences.

"She reads *tarot* cards. That's kinda suspicious if you ask me." We heard her saying. Perhaps Kelsey's plan didn't backfire after all. She was adding fuel to the fire by spreading falsehoods about Natalie to anyone who was close enough to listen.

Natalie and I weren't blind to what was happening around us and we certainly weren't deaf. We both had a pretty good idea what the topic of conversation around The Pit was: Natalie. Gossip spread faster than wildfire in a town like Caldero and it was the only thing that traveled quickly around here.

"What the hell?" Natalie said.

The hushed voices weren't so low enough we couldn't hear the town's resident gossip committee chattering about Natalie and her recent escapades about the town. Folks had remained silent until Kelsey riled them all up. I turned and glanced around the restaurant, noting the customers were staring at us right back in return. "I don't know. But I have a feeling the one responsible is Portia."

Since Portia hadn't made herself known in my presence those past few weeks, we just assumed she had been staying put—out of sight, out of mind. As it turned out—if you bought into the town gossip and their high probability of accuracy—Portia was certainly a woman who knew how to make an impression on a small unimposing town like Caldero.

"She must be coming out at night," Natalie determined. "It's the only possible explanation. I have been more tired than usual lately, but I just assumed it was stress. She's probably staying out all night doing God knows what or who all over town."

"I think you're right. So what do we do now? I can't very well chain you to the bed at night." I stopped and gave her my best sly grin. "Well, I could, but that would be purely for entertainment pleasure."

"*Wyatt*," she said with a giggle, resulting in more stares from the other tables. "It's bad enough Portia's whoring herself around town. I don't need the them thinking I'm a slut, too."

"That's the thing. They already do. Only they don't know it's your sister." I grimaced at the thought of Portia running around at night. It was still Natalie's body and that didn't sit well with me. Jokes aside, Natalie was mine and I wasn't about to let anyone take advantage of her. "We'll think of a way to put a stop to this."

She grabbed my hand, which was a far cry from a couple of months back when she shied away from my touch. "We have to do something and fast."

Even though we were in her aunt's restaurant, we'd had enough of the whispers so we decided to cut out early. I hated to think what the sisters were thinking right now, upon hearing the town gossip, but they kept themselves mostly in the kitchen, so perhaps they were spared. We passed by Tyler's table and he shot us a solemn nod, letting us know he had heard the whispering too but felt bad about it.

We didn't even say goodbye to Natalie's aunts, for fear they would figure out what was going on. It was probably better that we left before they got wind of what was going on and got angry and kicked everyone out. They didn't live far from The Pit, so we decided to enjoy the rare cool evening and walked back to her house.

I didn't want to talk about the rumors that were being spread at Natalie's expense, so I focused on something else. "Great trick back there, by the way. How'd you do it?" I finally got the nerve to ask her as we got closer to her house.

"Do what?" she asked.

"Manipulate the tarot readings. Either you made up the meaning of the cards or you some how tampered with the deck." I wasn't judging her by any means, in fact, I was actually quite impressed with how she handled Kelsey. "All of Kelsey's cards were upside down."

She laughed. "Don't you know that a good magician never shares her secrets?"

"Aha! So you did mess with the cards."

"No, I actually didn't, I swear. I have a knack for showing people what's right in front of them."

"That makes absolutely no sense. How can you possibly know what a person's future holds? I thought you only healed people."

"I'm not saying I know the future. The cards do. As a Healer, I am able to tap into various powers and I use the cards to channel that power. Knowing Kelsey the way you do, just how accurate was her reading?"

"Pretty dead on," I had to admit, not only impressed by the reading, but her ability to do other things besides heal.

"Can't you just see her becoming an aging beauty queen," she went on, "living in a trailer park, drinking wine out of a box because her life didn't end up the way she wanted it to?"

I could totally envision Kelsey ending up a bitter old woman, which made me think of my mother—her life didn't end up the way she had planned, either. She was a beauty queen herself once, who later became the mistress of a grand old house, with only her booze and memories keeping her company.

"I'm sorry, Wyatt. I spoke without thinking," she said, obviously thinking the same thing I was. "I didn't mean to imply your mom—"

"No, that's okay. I know what you meant. And yeah, I could totally see Kelsey's future end up like that."

Twenty-One

When she first told me about her special gifts, she'd said, "…every parish had a Great Priest."

I knew I couldn't go to the sisters, or even Carmen anymore, for advice, so I went to the one person I thought could come close to having the answers I sought, finding myself in front of St. Cecelia's to see Father Hilario. It'd been years since I'd set foot inside the church, but I didn't think the priest would turn me away. My presence would certainly raise questions, especially from Carmen, so I went early in the morning, on a weekday, so no one would know what I was up to.

Upon entering the church, I dipped my fingers in the bowl of holy water and made the sign of the cross. I may not have subscribed to the Catholic doctrine, but it was a familiar tradition and after everything I had learned these last few weeks, I figured it couldn't hurt.

St. Cecilia was one of the oldest Catholic churches in the area, having been built by the Irish settlers in the mid-1800's. The church was usually empty that time of the day, save one or two old ladies who were there to pray—the same old ladies I remembered when I came here as a child. They must come to St. Cecilia's every morning to pray for all us sinners, I assumed, because they couldn't possibly have committed that many sins worth repenting on a daily basis. They both ignored me, heads kept low as they prayed the rosary, as I walked up to the front of the church.

"Can I help you?" a voice asked from the far side of the pews.

Father Hilario had aged since the last time I saw him. The years had been kind to him, but he was definitely older looking, wiser somehow. His once salt and pepper hair had now turned almost all white. "It's Wyatt McKenna, do you remember me?"

"Of course, I remember all my parishioners. You haven't been here in a while," he noted.

I saw that one coming. "Sorry, Father, but you know how it goes." He didn't need to hear my opinion on organized religion.

"Don't worry son, Carmen prays enough for both of you. So tell me, what can I do for you today?"

I glanced over at the two women who were still praying. "Can we talk in private?"

"We can go to my office."

I followed the priest to the front where the altar stood where he led me to a hallway that extended toward the back of the church. As we entered his office, he motioned for me to sit.

"Now, tell me what's troubling you my son."

"Well, I don't really know where to start. You'll probably think I'm crazy, but I guess I should start at the beginning. It's about a girl."

Father Hilario smiled. "I see. And what do you want to know? Is this about relations outside the bonds of matrimony? A relationship between two young persons is a very serious commitment that should not be taken lightly."

Without having to look into a mirror for confirmation, I could feel my face flush red with embarrassment. The last thing I wanted to do was talk about my sex life—or lack thereof—with Father Hilario. "God no!" I exclaimed. "Oh, sorry, Father. I mean, no, it's not about that."

I could tell he was amused by my nervousness. "Then you will need to be a little more specific so that I may help you."

Obviously, there was no easy way to explain the entire story, so I decided the best approach was quick and painless. "Do you know anything about the Great Priests?"

For a moment Father Hilario just stared at me, his amused expression fading. I had a pretty good idea that he knew exactly what I was talking about.

"What, dear child, do you know of the Great Priests?" he asked, not committing himself to an answer.

"That they exist. I know about the Healers too."

"I'm not sure I know what you're asking." He didn't deny anything I just said.

"It's Natalie Betancourt. She's in trouble. There's got to be a way to help her." At this point, I knew I didn't have to rehash the series of events that led me here. "Look Father, I know you know what's going on." I didn't know this for sure. I only hoped he didn't call my bluff.

The old priest nodded. "Then I'm sure you know that there's nothing that can be done to save her. There is nothing I, nor her aunts can do."

"That's not acceptable. You guys put Portia in her, now get her out."

"It's not that simple."

"I think it is."

"We cannot allow Portia to roam free. That is not an option."

First Carmen refused to help and now the priest. "Oh, I get it. What you're saying is, you would rather have Natalie suffer than to let her sister go. It's not that you can't help her, you just won't."

"Son, I know—"

"No, you don't know," I said, a little more harsh than I intended it to come out. "I thought if I came by here, you'd be willing to offer up some advice. I can see that I've wasted my time. If you're not going to help, then I'm just going to have to figure this one out for myself. I don't know if you've heard the town gossip, but Portia is starting to come out more often. Pretty soon she's going to take over and there's nothing Natalie can do to stop it. Don't you care about that?" Maybe if he knew how much of a threat Portia was, he'd be forced to take some action.

"I don't think you understand the ramifications of getting involved. Natalie is the only one strong enough to hold her sister. The forces that Portia has acquired has proven more powerful than we could have ever imagined and if she were to be expelled from Natalie's body, it would put humanity at a great risk. There is no precedent for this, so we had to do what was necessary in order to contain her."

"Even at the expense of Natalie's life? You know Portia is getting stronger. Pretty soon she'll take over Natalie's body and you won't be able to do anything about it, anyway. Isn't that enough of a reason to find another way to control Portia?"

"Our hands our tied with respect to this situation. We are tasked only with guiding and protecting the Healers as we become aware of them. The Great Priests do not meddle in the forces that are beyond their control. It was in that extreme case that the priests intervened. I am sorry."

"Then why is the church bound to protect her kind? Why bother if you can't step in to help?" As soon as I asked the question, I instantly knew the answer. The only reason they were involved was to guard over them. They'd set themselves up in a prime position to serve as watchdogs. It had nothing to do with the knowledge or guidance they offered healers like Natalie, but rather they wanted to keep a watchful eye on them.

He didn't say anything for a long while. I didn't know if this was a sign that the issue was closed, whether he was going to consider my request for help, or whether he was trying to find a way to let me down gently, which would probably still end up being patronizing no matter how much he tried to sugarcoat it.

As I sat there waiting for him to say something, I began to feel lightheaded from the lingering scent of incense. How could he stand to be in the church all day with that thick, musky perfume in the air?

Father Hilario cleared his throat. "The only way to dispose of Portia is to kill the corporeal body that contains her soul. Whether it be her own or Natalie's. But we cannot and will not end either of their lives. It could become a possibility if Portia's soul continues to gain more power, but for now it is not an option."

"You knew that and you put her in Natalie anyway." I slammed my hand against his desk in a fit of anger. It wasn't a question, but I still couldn't believe what I was hearing. These priests knew containing Portia would ultimately lead to Natalie's death and they did it anyway. Though I probably shouldn't take it out on the old priest. It wasn't really his fault. He just happened to be the one sitting in front of me at the moment.

"You'd be best to keep your voice down. *I* didn't do anything. I am just the messenger, my son. Nothing can be solved by allowing yourself to get angry." Father Hilario reached beneath his desk and pulled out a box not much larger than a cigar box. He reached into the box and pulled out a book that looked older than any bound text I'd ever seen. "You know, you remind me a lot of your father. He used to get worked up about the things he was passionate about."

His last statement caught me off guard. "What do you know of my father?"

It was the briefest of flinches, but it was definitely a flinch that crossed the priest's face. "He used to be a parishioner here. I remember him fondly."

"Oh." For a second I thought he was going to tell me more about my father, like maybe why he decided to leave me and my mother—I guess not all people confess their sins before heading out to start a new chapter in their life. Not that Father Hilario would be able to tell me even if he had.

Father Hilario placed the book in my hands.

"What's this?"

"It is the text which explains the history and evolution of the The Ancient Ones. It might help you understand more about Natalie and her true nature. I cannot loan you the book, of course, as it cannot leave the confines of the church. To be quite honest, I shouldn't even have allowed you know of its existence, but since you know too much already…" His voice trailed off. "You may come look upon it anytime you wish. It may not prove to help you in your quest, but at least some of your questions can be answered."

"I'm guessing it doesn't explain how to exorcise Portia out of Natalie?"

"No, my son. How the Great Priests decided to handle Portia was a result of many magical forces at play. It was a last resort on their part, and the ritual was never recorded. There was no need, as we never expected to reverse what had been done. It was not, and is still not, a consideration that will be entertained."

"I see," I said, resigned to the fact that the Church refused to help.

"You are welcome here anytime you wish to read from the book. Or to pray."

Twenty-Two

I'd never known the De León sisters to pay a personal visit to Carmen at the house. If anything, it was always the other way around. It was Carmen who either requested healing herbs or would go directly to them if she had a problem she couldn't solve or client she couldn't help on her own. Something was definitely wrong if Amelia and Ester were coming over to the house. At that hour of the night, I knew it wasn't just a social visit.

I snuck out of my room, taking advantage of the outdoor stairs, careful not to make a sound as I quietly walked across the balcony to get a better view of the scene below. Though I didn't know why I bothered.

Once Carmen had led them to the back of the house and the women had made themselves comfortable on the back porch, I crouched down near the railing so I could hear their conversation. I was sure that if Carmen or the sisters found me sneaking around, I knew I'd be in deep shit. Just what exactly were they doing out there?

The night was still enough for me to overhear their conversation from where they were situated down below. The three women spoke Spanish, but even as rusty as mine was, I could understand it a hell of a lot more than I could speak it. They spoke a little too fast to keep up with everything that was being said, but I was able to get an idea of what they were saying: Natalie was in *mucho* trouble.

The whispered jumble of English and Spanish was beginning to make more sense to me the longer I eavesdropped. Since I'd been home, my Spanish was starting to come back to me. From what I was able to make out, they were going to do a *limpia*—a spiritual cleansing.

I could hear the crunch of gravel coming from the side of the house as a dark silhouette formed on the back porch. There was no moon tonight, so the nigh sky was dark, offering no illumination, making it hard to make out who it was joining the three older women. But as the shadowed figure got closer to the house, the dim light from the porch provided a better view of the person: she was tall, slender, with long dark hair. It was Natalie.

Was she a part of this eclectic ensemble, or was she the one receiving the cleaning? But I already knew the answer.

Fascinated, I watched in earnest over what the three women were doing in preparation for the cleansing. Natalie just sat on the back porch swing in silence, watching the women work. I didn't know what she was thinking, just sitting there, but I could tell she was scared. She had to be to resort to this Old World ritual.

I continued to watch in amazement as Ester held an egg above Natalie's head and began to sweep it down in a circular motion around the rest of her body while Carmen began to pray. Carmen was still praying as Ester repeated the process of sweeping the egg around Natalie's body.

It was only when Carmen stopped chanting that Ester then took the egg and made the sign of the cross with it on Natalie's forehead. I took it as a sign that the real portion of the cleansing was about to take place. Only Ester wasn't done. She began to make the sign of the cross with the egg over all of Natalie's body parts: her chest, the back of her chest, her palms, and then finally, the soles of her feet.

When it was all over, Amelia walked toward the three women with a glass bowl full of water. Ester nodded and broke the egg on the rim of the bowl and emptied the shell in the water. Because the bowl was made of clear glass, I was able to see what the others saw.

The color red.

Blood was mixed in with the egg whites and yolk. Even I knew it wasn't a good sign. It didn't take a faith healer to realize that the contents of the broken egg were symbolic of something—only I didn't know what that something was exactly.

The De León sisters made the sign of the cross (again) and Carmen just kept staring at the bowl and began to chant once more, only this time it was a different prayer. All the while Natalie kept her head down, oblivious to the scene the three older women were making, as if she had already expected the outcome of the ritual.

Even from my distance above, I was still able to see that the egg had split in two: one pristine yellow yolk and one yolk soaked in blood. Growing up in rural Texas, with many a friend or relative that raised hens, the superstitions that came with a double yolk egg varied with who you spoke to. It was either a sign of good luck or impending death. In this case, I figured it was the latter, the way the old women were carrying on about the meaning.

If what they were saying was true, it didn't look like Natalie ever had a fighting chance. But I wasn't going to give up. There had to be a way for them to get Portia out, even if it meant going to the Great Priests for answers. I wasn't going to lose Natalie, not by giving up.

Even from my balcony view, I could tell Natalie didn't seem too concerned over the outcome of the ritual.

It was as if she had already come to terms with her fate. But if she knew that, why did she even go through with the cleansing? She had to know that something as common as a *limpia* wouldn't be enough to do much of anything.

But what did I know? I was the one without faith.

Twenty-Three

Late one Tuesday evening, finding myself with nothing to do for a change, I found myself alone at Hector's. Natalie had decided to help her aunts and pitch in at The Pit, Ty was on a date with some girl he picked up at the gas station, and Carmen was doing God knows what with her new batch of healing herbs.

As I sat down and looked at my reflection in the mirror behind the bar, I thought back to a time when we came here back in high school. We thought we were so cool back then, but in reality, we were just a bunch of dumb kids. The bar was actually named after the owner himself and Hector used to turn a blind eye when it came to us drinking under age. It was his philosophy that our parents were the ones responsible for keeping us in line, not him—he had a business to run and a family to support.

Hector slid a bottle of Shiner onto the bar before I even placed my order, he knew me that well. The mustard orange label was a sight for sore eyes and a temporary cure for heavy heart. I was quite content to sit at the bar, nursing my beer, when I felt someone watching me. I turned to my left to find the source. It was Chris, the owner from the dance hall. We exchanged nods acknowledging each other across the bar. He seemed to hesitate before moving down the bar to sit next to me.

"It isn't easy, is it?" Chris asked.

"What isn't?"

"Being with someone you care about with your whole heart, and it breaks when others don't understand."

I hadn't realized Chris paid much attention to the comings and goings of the town, but then I remembered he used to be in law enforcement. Being observant was probably second nature to him. "You're talking about Kiki," I said. It couldn't be easy living in a small town with a former stripper who insisted on wearing body glitter to shop for groceries.

Chris took a swig of his beer. "The one and only. There really is only one like her in the world," he said with obvious pride when speaking of his girlfriend. "And of course, I'm talking about your Natalie. Quite a catch you got yourself there."

"Thanks," I said, confused. I wasn't making the connection between Kiki and Natalie. Though I was pretty sure he wasn't immune to the town gossip surrounding Natalie. I only hoped he wasn't buying into it.

He continued, "It's been my experience that when people make a fuss over someone, it's usually because that person is different. Folks in a small town like Caldero don't like different, Wyatt. They don't like change either for that matter.

"I know they talk about me and Kiki. And at first, I took offense to it until Kiki told me that what others think don't matter. I finally took her advice and began to enjoy living here with her by my side. A man can't ask for anything better than that.

"Most folks around here wouldn't know it by looking at her, but my Kiki is one of the strongest persons I've ever met. She could even teach some of my former colleagues a thing a two about courage. She's also pretty damned smart, too. It's because of her the dance hall's in the black for the first time in years. Had nothing to do with me. I'm just a glorified bouncer."

I understood what he was finally getting at. The talk around town was that Natalie was no good. Portia's escapades around town didn't do much to bolster Natalie's reputation and because of that, Portia/Natalie's actions also reflected badly on me. No one seemed to look down on the De León sisters for their niece's lack of inhibitions, as—

according to the folks around town—they were blood kin and they had to take care of her ("poor dears," they whispers when the sisters weren't within earshot), but I on the other hand, had a choice.

"Why are you telling me this?"

"Oh, I don't know. Looked like you needed some friendly advice from someone who's been there." The former law man looked thoughtful for a moment before speaking again. "Women like ours are special.

"Now, I'm not saying they're the same. Hell, I hardly even know your girlfriend, but I've seen that same kind of spark in her that I see in my Kiki. I guess my point is, don't let others dictate who you see or what you do. And if you find that special someone, don't ever let her go."

There wasn't anything anyone could do or say to make me change my mind over wanting to be with Natalie, but hearing Chris say it out loud definitely put things in perspective.

"Thanks for the advice."

"No problem."

"So why'd you leave the DEA?" No one had ever gotten the full story, at least not to my knowledge. I'm surprised the esteemed members of the gossip circle hadn't gotten around to it. They were usually on top of anything that had the slightest hint of scandal.

He hesitated a briefly before answering. "There was a pretty bad case I worked on a few years back. Saw some shit you wouldn't believe. I finally decided my job wasn't worth my life. Plus, Kiki and I wanted a fresh start. So we moved to Caldero. She was in the entertainment business as I'm sure you already know, so when we found out the dance hall was for sale, we snatched it up."

"Is that what happened to your face? That bad case you worked on, I mean." I'd always been curious as to where he got the deep scars that ran from his left temple all the way down to his chin. It looked like a bobcat mauled the one side of his face.

"You could say that."

"Every consider plastic surgery?" In truth, the scars weren't so bad that they warranted surgery, but as a future med student, it was a legitimate question.

He laughed. "Nah, I like to consider them as well-deserved battle scars. Got them the night I finally made my move on Kiki. I don't want to erase any part of that night," he said. "Besides, she thinks they make me look sexy."

We spent rest of the evening sitting at the bar in silence, enjoying the beer that kept replenishing itself, thanks to Hector. When I finished my fourth bottle of Shiner, I finally said my goodbyes to Chris, wishing I could stay longer to shoot the shit. "Hey, thanks, man."

"Anytime. And hey, for what it's worth, if you ever need anything, just say the word."

"I'll keep that in mind."

Twenty-Four

Talking with Chris got me thinking about my relationship with Natalie.

With two freshly brewed cups of coffee secured in the truck's cup holders I'd installed a few years back, I arrived at the fading, purple structure as soon as I could without causing any alarm given the early morning hour. My intentions for the day included a little field trip which would allow me and Natalie to get out of Dodge—in a Ford pick-em-up truck. We needed time away from Caldero and I knew just the place to take her.

Breakfast didn't make itself, so I knew I didn't have to worry about the De León sisters objecting to my taking Natalie out this particular outing, as they would already be over at the restaurant preparing for the breakfast rush. It was Natalie I had to convince. I really didn't think they would have objected to Natalie going out of town with me, but I didn't want to take the chance they'd say no.

"What in the world are you doing here at this ungodly hour?" Natalie asked, obviously still trying to wake up after I banged on the door for her to let me in at five in the morning. "You scared me to death. I thought the cops were here to tell me something happened to my aunts."

I wasn't completely insensitive, which was why I'd arrived bearing pre-morning provisions: breakfast taquitos and coffee. They weren't of the same quality of a De León breakfast taco, but it was sustenance nonetheless and we were going to need it for the trip on which we were about to embark. "Sorry. I didn't mean to freak you out. I came by because we're going on a trip."

"I don't remember signing up for a road trip," she said, eying me curiously. I was pleased I'd piqued her interest.

"Trust me, where I'm about to take you, you'll have so much fun, you'll be thanking me later."

She frowned. "What about my aunts? I can't just pick up and leave without letting them know where I am. I don't want them to worry."

I was prepared for the excuse. "If you want, we can stop by the restaurant and let them know of our plans. Or you can always leave them a note."

Natalie mulled her options over. "I'll leave them a note," she finally decided. "But before I do, what are the plans exactly? Where are we going?"

"Can't say, but you might want to pack an overnight bag. Unless you want to drive back in the middle of the night. Either way, we won't be coming back until tomorrow."

"Do you really think I'm going to agree to go with you, an overnight trip I might add, without first knowing where we're going?"

"Yup. That's the plan. Look, I promise to behave myself. I just thought with all that's happened, you could use a little time away. Oh, and you have to decide now. We're burning daylight hours."

She thought about it. I could see the silent debate going through her head as she considered my offer. "You know what? Screw it, I'm game. When do we leave?"

"Now."

"Are you kidding? I just woke up!" Her hands went straight to her head, smoothing out her tousled bed hair. "I need some time to get ready."

"You have ten minutes. Like I said, we're burning daylight," I said, anxious to get a move on. Every minute we spent talking was time lost on the highway.

"It's not even dawn yet," she pointed out.

"A mere technicality. Ten minutes," I said again, pointing to the staircase to indicate she needed to get a move on.

((

Once we were on the road, I couldn't contain my excitement and revealed our destination. I don't think she believed me at first, because she appeared genuinely surprised when we drove passed the Welcome to Louisiana tourism sign just after crossing Orange, Texas into Cajun Country.

Another reason for leaving before dawn, aside from it being a seven hour road trip, was the heat. There was no escaping the Gulf Coast humidity, no matter which state line you crossed. Fortunately, the morning was just cool enough—just barely—to get us a few hours of comfortable driving time before the real heat set in my barely functioning air-conditioned scrap-metal excuse for a truck (which I loved). And not once did Natalie complain about the sweat trickling down her neck or the liquid beads forming above her brow. But we made good time, avoiding most of the traffic on the interstate.

"I can't believe you drove us all the way to Louisiana!" Natalie exclaimed. "We could have just gone to Austin if you wanted a weekend away, you know."

"What's the fun in that? If you want to really let loose and have a good time, you go to N'awlins," I drawled as the locals do, pleased by her excitement.

She could only shake her head in amazement. "I can't believe we're actually here."

Natalie probably never traveled much as a child. "I know it's not much of a destination place, but I figured we needed to let loose and this was the one place I could think of."

"It's perfect. I've always wanted to spend some time here. To see the architecture, visit all the places I'd only read about, stroll around the Garden District, ride on the St. Charles streetcar, visit Marie Laveau's resting place. I want to do it all!"

She was so giddy with excitement I knew I had made the right decision to bring her here. To my adoptive home—the place I had ultimately chosen to jumpstart my new life. They say home is where the heart is, and by bringing Natalie here, I finally understood the meaning behind the sentiment—even if only for a day.

"And here I thought you'd be interested in going to Bourbon Street and getting wasted on hurricanes," I mocked. "You realize we'll only be in town for a day, right?"

She laughed along with me. "So you said. And don't even think for a second I'm doing anything to earn those beads I've heard so much about."

I grinned at the mental picture of Natalie showing a little skin to the locals. It was a lovely image at that. "Nah, that's only during Mardi Gras. Well, officially, that is. But don't worry, I won't let you take your top off. No matter how drunk I get you." But we both knew I was joking. With Portia and her penchant for alcohol, we knew we had to keep the booze at a minimum.

She lightly punched me in the arm. "Thanks for nothing. So, where to first?"

"It's your day, you pick. But I need to make a quick stop at some point." I didn't offer any more information than that. For the time being, it was best to let her assume I had some errands to run while we were in town. For all intents and purposes this was my home, so I knew it wouldn't come off as a strange request.

"Sure. How about about some food first? I'm a little hungry."

"Music to my ears. Aside from your aunts' kitchen, New Orleans is one of the best places to indulge in culinary bliss."

"Lead the way."

New Orleans had no shortage of places you could go to if you were looking to impress a girl who was unfamiliar with the city, but I thought better of it. Most places in the Quarter were there more for ambiance than the food itself. Truth be told, not many menus in town held a candle to her aunts' dishes (or Carmen's), so I wasn't sure how impressed she'd actually be. In the end, I took her to one of my favorite haunts, Domilise's on Annunciation Street, a little out of the way place where they served the best oyster po'boys.

It was still fairly early for lunch and I was pleased to find the place with only a few folks in line a head of us. We took a plastic number and waited to place our order. Natalie was amazed by the no-nonsense customer service and decided it was all worth the wait and effort when our order was called. In between a mouthful of fried oysters and french bread she said, "This is amazing. I've never had anything quite like this before. Quite a little hole in the wall, isn't it?"

What I didn't tell her was that the little hole in the wall oyster shack wasn't too far from Big Momma Ledoux's shop in Central City, located in the lower end of Uptown New Orleans. After witnessing the failed cleansing attempt and getting absolutely nowhere with Father Hilario, I figured the old voodoo woman was our last chance. Only this time, I wouldn't get my hopes up. No one was willing to help us thus far, but it was still worth a shot.

☾

We stood in front of the little voodoo shop. Home to Big Momma Ledoux.

"How do you even know about this place like this? It doesn't seem like the kind of place you'd frequent, with you being anti-faith and all," Natalie inquired.

Standing there in front of the dilapidated shop, I remembered that day at Big Momma's like it was yesterday. "Before I left for Caldero, I came here looking for something to write about for a research paper." I never did find anything useful for my paper, but instead I found Natalie. I had convinced myself that the pull I had felt to return to Caldero was due in part to Big Momma. Without her urging, I doubt I would have ever met Natalie. Then again, perhaps it was all just happenstance.

"Why are we here now?"

It was a damn good question. "Honestly, I was kind of hoping Big Momma Ledoux could help. I'm willing to try anything. Aren't you?" I was really hoping she'd be on board with coming to see the voodoo priestess and not get mad now that I revealed the true purpose of our trip. Natalie had made it quite clear she believed her situation hopeless, but there was always the chance she hadn't given up quite yet. And in my heart, I hope she hadn't given up on us. Because for me, that's what this was all about. If she gave up on herself, there would never be an *us*.

"I thought you didn't believe in that kind of thing."

I pulled her close to me, close enough to smell the light beer she'd consumed over lunch. "I'm willing to have a little faith if it means helping you get out of this mess. Besides, how can I not believe after meeting you?"

"Good point. Let's go in and meet this Big Momma woman."

I breathed a sigh of relief, thankful she was willing to meet the old voodoo shopkeeper. Even though I now believed in Natalie and her powers, I still didn't know if I could bring myself to believe the whole voodoo crap the old woman peddled. She could be a fake. For all I knew, the feeling in my stomach could have been indigestion, not some magical force pulling me toward Caldero. Natalie herself had said there was a difference between someone like her and someone who dabbled in the black arts, but it was worth a try.

The bell chimed as we entered Big Momma Ledoux's storefront. Upon hearing the bell, Big Momma waddled over from behind the black curtain to see who dared come visit the little voodoo shop, very much like she had the first time I entered her store. This time around, she was happy to see me, I could tell. "I see you heeded my advice, boy," the old woman crooned when she saw the two of us approach the counter.

"Sure, I went home. No biggie."

As much as Big Momma seemed pleased to see us, she got down to business in a matter of seconds. "How can I help you?"

Just what did I expect Big Momma to do? Aside from dragging Natalie all the way here to meet with some old voodoo woman, I hadn't the foggiest notion so I was honest in my response. "I'm not sure exactly. I guess we came to see if you could help us." I kept it vague, just in case, Natalie didn't want me divulging her secrets.

She grunted and set her eyes on Natalie. "Let me see your palm, *chère*," she said.

Natalie did as she was told and held out her palm over the counter for the old woman to inspect.

"Just as I thought. They be two souls," she said, tracing the edge of Natalie's palm with her plump finger. "They struggle. Only one will triumph."

Without saying another word, she went back behind the black curtain. Natalie and I exchanged glances and waited to see if she'd return.

The voodoo priestess came back from beyond the curtain and spoke directly to me. "I anticipated your arrival," she said. "Here." She pressed a small leather pouch into my palm. "Take this and keep it with you."

The pouch looked like some sort of gris-gris charm I'd often heard about, but from what I'd gathered, a gris-gris was considered to be a form of black magic. I was afraid to look inside it. What if it contained human hair, or even teeth? Just holding the damn thing gave me the creeps.

"What makes you think this will help? We didn't even tell you what the problem is."

"You ask too many questions, *cher*. Just take it and keep it on you at all times," she instructed again.

"Thanks," I said, placing the offending pouch in my pants pocket. "What do we owe you?" I may not have put much credence in what she said, but I wasn't going take advantage of her. She did have a business to run after all.

"It be a gift," she said. "Your presence here is payment enough. Now, go."

"But isn't there—" I was going to ask her about Natalie and if she could help, but she cut me off.

"No. There be nothing else I can do for her," she said, already knowing that I was going to ask.

Puzzled, we left the shop with the voodoo lady yelling after us. "Keep it on you at all times!"

Outside of the shop and out of earshot, I asked Natalie, "What do you know about voodoo? Is this thing black magic or what?"

Natalie shrugged. "It's not something my aunts nor I have ever dealt with. Our magic comes from within. We use tools like the tarot or herbs to conduct spells and such, mostly to make our clients comfortable, but something like that," she said, pointing at the small pouch, "I'm afraid it's out of my realm."

"I was afraid you'd say that," I said, rubbing the soft worn leather against my fingers. "What do you think? Do I take her advice?" Since we never got around to telling the old woman about why were there in the first place, her little bag of charms would just have to do.

"At this point, why not?"

Now that we'd paid our visit to Big Momma Ledoux, which was the main reason for our trip, Natalie and I took advantage of the city and had some much-needed fun. For a few hours, we forgot about Portia, all things related to magic, and all that awaited us in Caldero upon our return.

Twenty-Five

It was a few days later and the aunts had finally forgiven us for taking off to New Orleans. I didn't honestly think they'd actually be that upset about our trip, but they certainly weren't happy when we returned.

We were at The Pit and the sisters asked me and Natalie to lock up after closing. I had a feeling they had a few appointments they had to keep back at home. I had kept the knowledge of the book Father Hidalgo had shown me a secret until I could make heads or tails of it myself. I wanted to learn more of what Natalie was before I told her about the book, but it was now time for me to tell her what I knew. And I couldn't think of a better place than in the privacy of the closed restaurant where no one would bother us.

"What's that?" She asked, pointing at the large book in my hands.

"Your history. Or rather a skewed version of it." I plopped the leather bound text on the table.

"Where did you get it?" It was obvious she had never seen or even heard of the book. She picked it up and flipped the pages, then ran her hands over the intricate details on the front worn cover.

"Father Hidalgo."

"You went to see Father Hidalgo? When? What did he say? And he just gave this to you?"

"Yes and no. Yes, I went to see him a couple of weeks ago and no, he didn't exactly allow me to take it."

"I can't believe you did that." She kept her voice even, but I could tell she was pissed. "Wyatt, it wasn't your place to talk to him, especially about me. And secondly, you had no right to take that from him."

I couldn't believe what I was hearing. Didn't she want to know more about her kind? And what bothered me most was that no one had ever bothered to show her the book. "Aren't you even the least bit curious as to what it says? Don't you even want to know why they kept something like this from you?"

"Of course I want to know. I didn't even know something like this existed. But it wasn't yours to take. And from a priest!"

Natalie quietly browsed through the book, stopping to read a page here and there. "Have you read any of this yourself?"

The book was about her history, her life, and even though she hadn't read the text herself, I had taken it like a kid stealing a sibling's diary. "Not all of it. Look, I'm sorry. I just thought that if I read it, I could understand you a little better. You hadn't been exactly forthcoming with information at the time."

"Did it mention anything about how to get rid of Portia?" This time, her voice lingered on the verge of forgiveness.

"No, it didn't. That's what's confusing. It doesn't say much of anything at all."

She kept flipping through the pages. "Wait, what's this?" She began to gently tug at the back of the book.

"What?" I moved in for a closer look.

"There's pages that don't match the rest of the text," she pointed out. "See? It's not even bound together with the others. The writing is different too."

"How did I miss that?" I pored over that book and hadn't even noticed. I wonder what else I might have missed.

"It looks like the pages were stuck together," I said. "Let's read what it says."

In our quest to answer the similarities (or differences) between the beliefs of shamanism in archaic texts, our search has uncovered numerous religious beliefs regarding the supernatural powers of the Healers. The stories and myths revolving around such superstitious folk tales are quite telling: the curanderas of Mexico, the witch doctors of Africa, the shaman culture of Mesoamerica, the Navajo Hatalii's, and the Táltos legends of Hungary. The latter being the most powerful or supernatural of the beings in question which bears a close resemblance to the Healers we know of as of today's writing. The supernatural being that we have now come to call Healers are the oldest if not the most archaic beings in our findings known to date aside from The Ancient Ones.

We have now concluded that The Ancient Ones were in direct contact with God in the womb. It is presumed that in that prenatal state they were given direct knowledge on the powers of healing. Once born and armed with this knowledge, The Ancient Ones were able to cure the human race, in both body and the soul. The Healers, we have now come to find, are direct descendants of this special race.

Other beings that we have come in contact with throughout our studies are as equally as important, such as seers, prophets, and diviners. However, those we consider Healers have distinguished themselves from the others by their curious and distinguishing characteristics.

It was a unanimous decision on the part of our council to send Father Thomas to collect more up-to-date information on the mystical nature of the Healers. His research was limited, but not without merit. What he found was a collection of texts and artifacts to support our belief in the creation of the Healers. An offspring of The Ancient Ones, born of a human, the Healers are of the same vein.

It is with great importance to watch over the Healers as they continue to progress among us over time in this modern day society. Our quest for research and absolution in this matter is of grave importance. Our mission to watch and observe will continue.

Father Dimitri 1990

"What do you make of all this? And who are Father Thomas and Father Dmitri?" I asked.

"They're most likely members of the Keepers of the Watch."

"You mean you don't know? Neither of those names sound familiar to you?" I asked.

Natalie shook her head. "I know of the council, but none of them personally. They tend to keep their distance."

"So let me get this straight. These priests, the ones who are bound to protect you and your kind, have spend centuries researching your history, yet they keep their distance from you. They don't communicate with you, nor do they appear to have any desire whatsoever to keep in contact with you. How the hell are you supposed to know anything about your life and history if they keep themselves closed off?"

"You said it yourself. You found nothing of value in that book. So I'm assuming there's nothing in there I don't already know."

"That's not the point and you know it." Why was I the only one getting so upset? It wasn't my life we were arguing about—it was hers.

Twenty-Six

Somewhere in the jungles of Brazil...

"Father Thomas, there is a message for you from the States."

The priest took the telegram from the young barefooted young man who served as his guide.

SHE IS GETTING STRONGER. THE TIME HAS COME. REQUESTING ASSISTANCE. PLEASE COME HOME. FATHER HILARIO.

He had been afraid the girl would not be able to contain the soul for long. When he left the States, he made a promise never to return and he didn't intend on breaking that vow. There was nothing he could do to help and reflected and prayed on what he could not do.

His time in the jungles of Brazil was his penance, and he had every intention to serve out his sentence in servitude to the Lord, as payment for his past transgressions.

Father Thomas crumpled the telegraph and fed it to the open fire.

"What was it Father?" The boy asked.

"Nothing."

Twenty-Seven

Natalie and I were running out of options. While she was resigned at first to allow her sister's soul to reside in her, she now realized we had to find a way to get her out. I knew the Great Priests weren't going to step in and do what was right, so I had to turn elsewhere. Carmen and Big Momma were of no help, and I was pretty sure her aunts were out of ideas if they hadn't come up with any since that night of the cleansing ritual.

I considered what was left. I was taking a big chance in telling Tyler about Natalie, but I was out of ideas. If Natalie knew I was about to divulge her secrets to Tyler, she'd probably never forgive me, but if it my plan worked out the way I hoped, maybe she'd understand what I was about to do. Act first, ask forgiveness later.

Tyler's parents were home, so I couldn't risk telling him anything there, so I called him up and asked him to meet me at Hector's. The bar was usually dead this time of day, so we could talk freely without fear of anyone eavesdropping. The place attracted a rather mixed bag in the early afternoon hours, so if anyone was drinking at this hour of the day they wouldn't remember overhearing our conversation anyway come the following morning.

I got there before Tyler, which wasn't a big surprise since he usually ran late. Content to sip my beer and wait, I thought about all the ways I would broach the subject of Natalie with my best friend.

"Yo. So what's up?" Tyler slid onto the stool next to mine. "You sounded serious on the phone."

I still didn't know how I was going to tell him, but I figured it was too late to back out now. "I gotta tell you something, but don't freak out, okay?"

"Sure, we're like brothers man, you know you can tell me anything." Under any other circumstance, this would've been true, but this wasn't your run-of-the-mill secret.

"I need your help, but first I need to know I can count on you." That was it, the defining moment where I find out who my true friends really are. I knew it was a risk confiding in him, but it was a risk worth taking.

"You name it, you got it," Tyler said.

"Natalie's in trouble."

"I *knew* something was going on with that girl. You didn't knock her up, did you?" He eyed me with concern.

If he only knew about our nonexistent sex life. "Ty, focus. No, she's not pregnant. It's worse than that." I went into everything that's happened the last couple of months, the hijacking of Natalie's body, the Great Priests, Big Momma Ledoux—everything. As I began to recount my fantastic tale, I gauged Tyler's reaction to see if I should go further. He just sat there intrigued, hanging on every word.

"Whoa, that's some shit you've got yourself in to. You're right, a baby would have been better." I gave him a stern look. "What? It's true. Okay, so what do you need me to do?"

No matter what, deep down I knew in the end I could count on my best friend. We sat there in a confounded silence. Me, over whether or not it was a good idea to confide Natalie's secret, and Tyler, I'm sure, over whether or not I was crazy.

"So you're saying she's some kind of super healer witch and her sister has invaded her body?" Tyler finally asked.

"That just about sums it up," I said.

"Dude, that's just like Invasion of the Body Snatchers," he said, impressed.

I really wasn't be surprised by Tyler's reaction, considering Tyler was a huge horror buff. This was the same guy who was proud of the fact that he'd seen *Texas Chainsaw Massacre* over twenty times—each film adaptation. So I was pretty sure he was loving every minute of this.

"I guess, but trust me, this is no movie. Do you remember that day when I caught Natalie over at your place? That wasn't Natalie, it was her sister Portia. That's why I had to get her out of there."

Tyler sat there, momentarily stunned. "No shit? Why didn't you just say so? Why'd you wait 'til now to tell me all this? I would have understood."

I found this hard to believe, yet there I was, telling him everything. "Really? Would you have?"

"Okay, no. But I would stand by you no matter what. You know that. Even if it's something as crazy as what you're telling me now."

In hindsight, maybe I underestimated my friend, then again knowing him as well as I do, I knew he'd be game for anything that had freaky written all over it. He's right though, I should have told him about Natalie sooner, but I just didn't know how. I mean, how do you tell your best friend that the woman you love is some kind of supernatural witch that plays host to her evil sister? "I'm telling you now. So are you going to help us or not?"

Tyler downed the last of his beer before before giving me his answer. "Just say the word." He then looked over at Hector and signaled him over. "I'm gonna need another beer."

Tyler's acceptance and willingness to help us gave me hope. No one else was willing to help us, but this was a start and I was grateful. Now, I wasn't naive enough to think we could fight Natalie's sister all on our own, but every ounce of muscle-power helped. With Tyler's build, after a years of playing college ball, coupled with his strength, and most importantly, his sex appeal, could be an asset to us. And my best friend was just cocky enough to believe he could do just about anything.

For the rest of the afternoon we devised a plan that played on Portia's weakness for men. With Tyler being a perfect compliment—being a man-whore himself—we figured it was the best course of action. Now all I had to do was convince Natalie that we were going to take matters into our own hands and defeat her sister ourselves.

☾

Natalie was livid.

I stopped by her house while her aunts were at the restaurant, and told her what I'd done. I knew she'd be upset, but I wasn't prepared for a fight.

"I can't believe you told Tyler," Natalie said. "What would you have done if he didn't believe you, or worse, thought you were crazy? If it wasn't about me, *I'd* think you were crazy."

She had every right to be angry, but she didn't know Tyler the way I did. "I knew I could count on him. I'm sorry I told him without discussing it with you first, but after that incident with Portia over at his house, I just had to tell him. Who knows when she'd decide to go after him again.? Besides, he's willing to help."

"Don't you get it? There's nothing anyone can do to fight this thing. She's getting stronger every day and pretty soon, I'm not going to be around to worth saving."

It pained me to hear her talk like that—in a twisted way, it was like I was losing her already. "You can't think that way." I wanted to tell her that I loved her, but I didn't want to scare her off even more. As it was, she was hesitant to be around me, but I couldn't control the way I felt about her. "Are you giving up? Because I sure as hell haven't."

"I'm not giving up," she said, finally calming down. "I just don't thing the three of us are equipped to tackle something like this. If the Great Priests say they can't stop her, how are we supposed to?"

"Screw the priests. Don't *you* get it? They're not there to protect you and your kind. Their only mission is to watch and provide damage control. You said it yourself, if they allowed Portia to expose her powers, it would make it that much harder to guard your secret."

"Stop it," she cried. "You're wrong."

I lowered my voice. "I'm sorry, but think about it, Natalie. Do you really think they aren't helping because they can't or because they won't? That book of theirs should be proof enough that they merely regard you as nothing more than a research project."

"Just stop. You don't know that."

"I'm sorry," I said, feeling guilty for making her upset. It wasn't how I imagined this playing out when I came over. "I'm sorry for still believing in us."

Her eyes were still red from crying, but she recovered quickly. "And what about me? You keep insisting this is about us, but it's not. It's my life on the line, not yours."

Natalie was right. I was being selfish, only I had been too preoccupied with my own wants and needs to see it for what it really was. "I'm sorry." How many times was I going to have to apologize, I wondered.

She took my hand. "Your heart's in the right place and believe me, if there was anything I can do so that we can be together without the threat of my sister, I'd be all over it. I just think we've run out of options."

"What about your aunts? If we include them, maybe we'll have enough power to get rid of Portia. It could work, right?" I looked at her resigned expression and already knew the answer thinking back to that night outside on my front porch during their failed cleansing attempt. "So do you want to hear the plan Ty and I came up with?"

Natalie sighed. "Okay fine. Tell me, what's the plan?"

It was a start. "Well, it seems that Portia has a soft spot for our good friend Ty. We thought that if we could draw her out, by capitalizing on her attraction to Ty, we could talk her long enough to figure out what she wants from you."

"Seriously? That's the great plan you and Tyler came up with?"

"It seems to be her Achilles heel."

"What is?"

"Lust," I said with a grin. "Why not use it against her?"

We didn't actually think we'd be able to get rid of Portia that easily. At least, not without harming Natalie in the process, but we could at least try to pump as much information out of her—get an insight on what Portia actually wanted. The plan was simple: call Portia out and ask.

"I don't think is going to work. She may be trapped and indisposed at the moment, but I have a feeling she's always aware of what's going on," Natalie said.

Tyler was more optimistic on the subject. "Look, if it doesn't work then what's the worst that can happen? You get a good buzz on and the opportunity to flirt with a real man for a change," he joked.

The three of us decided that the best place to hold this unusual seance was in the De León's living room. That way, if we got busted, we wouldn't have to explain too much given that the sisters were already aware of the situation regarding Portia. If we'd done it back at my place, Carmen would have skinned my hide for sure.

"Okay, time to pick your poison," Tyler announced.

"Tequila," Natalie said. "If we're going to do this, let's do it right."

"Lime?" I asked.

"We're out of limes," she said. "But we have some oranges in the kitchen. That'll work."

As I went back to the kitchen to get the bottle of tequila and oranges for first stage of the plan, I began to wonder if this was going to work. The idea was to get Natalie drunk enough to draw Portia out. She always seemed to be at her strongest when Natalie's defenses were down, so we decided this would be the easiest way. It also didn't hurt that Portia was attracted to the opposite sex, arousal being her major weakness. With Tyler serving as wingman, I was somewhat certain we'd get a chance to have some face to face time with her. My uncertainly, however, lay with whether we'd actually accomplish anything by speaking to her.

Not wanting to be left out, Tyler and I also took a couple of shots with Natalie so she wouldn't be the only one drinking.

After several shots of tequila, it wasn't long before Tyler and I started to play the "Hey, do you remember the time?" game.

Twenty-Eight

"Sorry guys, I must have passed out," Portia said right after taking over Natalie's body. "What'd I miss?"

By this point, I had begun to notice the telltale signs whenever she made an appearance: rapid eye movement, disassociated speech, and most importantly, even though I was looking at Natalie's face, I was staring directly into Portia's eyes.

"Cut the crap. We know it's you, Portia."

There was no question that sardonic smile was Portia's. "Well, I expected as much. It's not like my sister to get snookered on booze, so I figured she was up to something. You wanna know a little secret?" She leaned in closer to where I was sitting on the couch and whispered in my ear, "I know most of what goes on in Natalie's body."

I stiffened at the thought. What else did she know?

If she was telling the truth, she not only knew her sister's thoughts, but it was as if she was seated front row center into my own. "I even know how much you turn her on, cowboy. Every touch, every embrace, I feel it too," she said. "And I'm also not above keeping tabs on you."

"How can you possibly do that?"

"Just because I'm stuck in my sister's body, doesn't mean I can't make arrangements to have you watched. Even in jail they allow you one phone call," she giggled.

The owl from my first night back came to mind. The one who almost hit my windshield coming home from the river. Amelia had explained they were *bruja negras*—evil witches in disguise. "You're the one that sent that big old barn owl to follow me."

She shrugged, not committing to anything. "Possibly. I have oodles and oodles of resources at my disposal," she chuckled again, enjoying the attention.

"Uh…" Tyler wanted to say something, probably trying to steer the conversation in another direction, but it was all he could muster given the topic. It might have been the first time he was ever tongue-tied in front of a woman.

I let the matter drop. There were more important things to discuss than whether or not she was having me followed. I went straight to the heart of the matter. "What is it you want, Portia?" I asked.

"What everybody wants," she said.

"And what's that?"

Portia dropped the smile. "Time," she said. "Because time's running out."

"Sorry, can't help you there." What exactly was she getting at?

"Oh, but that's where you're wrong, cowboy. You should care. You should care very, very, very much."

"How so?" I asked, careful not to let her push my buttons any more than she already had.

"When my time goes, so does hers. See, when her body gets tired of holding me in, and believe me, I can already feel the wear and tear, we both go poof." She made a flicking gesture in the air with her fingers to drive the point home.

I was afraid as much. "So what do you want," I asked again. "You knew we were here, so you came out for a reason. Surely it wasn't just to tell us that."

"You're all business, aren't you? Fine, I'll get down to the point. I need your help, cowboy. The way I see it, we're not on the same team, you and me, we're not even playing the same sport, but that doesn't mean we can't work together."

"To do what?"

"Get me out of this body."

I stiffened, hearing her talk about Natalie that way. As if she was just a host Portia was feasting on. But that's exactly what she was: a leech. A parasite that fed off

Natalie's energy and spirit. Did she have any love or regard for her own sister, I wondered.

"Aw, don't look so pained. Isn't that what you want, too? I can see it all over your face. That's why you planned this little meeting, isn't it?"

"To be honest, I was hoping you'd have an idea." Not that I was seriously entertaining the idea of helping Portia escape. I wanted her out of Natalie, sure, but the goal was still to find another vessel that could contain her —your basic run-of-the-mill "bait and switch." Only we still had no clue how were going to pull it off.

Portia slinked over to the coffee table and took a shot of tequila (no orange slice for her). "If I *knew*, I wouldn't need your help." She took another shot and finally took notice of Tyler, who sat there quietly watching us spar. "Well, hey there, sweet thing. I was wonderin' when I'd be seeing you again."

"Hey, Portia."

She gave Tyler another admiring glance. "Mmm, yum. I'll get to you later." Then she directed her attention back at me. "But first things first. What are you going to do about springing me out of this joint?"

"According to Natalie, you're supposed to be this grand black witch and you haven't figured out how to do it?"

Gone was the smirk on her face. "If I knew how, we wouldn't be having this conversation now would we? But

I'm happy to hear my dear sister thinks of me as someone so powerful."

"But not powerful enough to get yourself out," I reminded her once more.

"God dammit!" She cried to no one in particular. "I'm dealing with amateurs. *Humans*. You know nothing of our kind. I can't believe my sister would fall for someone like you. In fact," she said, walking closer to me. "I can't believe you'd fall for someone like her. She's always been somewhat of a downer. She should have been named Debbie."

"From where I'm standing, you're the one with problem," I said.

Not having any luck talking to me, Portia turned her attention back to Tyler. She walked behind the couch where he was seated and bent down far enough for him to hear her whisper. "I can tell just by looking at you, you're not an amateur, are you?"

His face turned a bright red at the suggestion. I'd never seen Tyler look so flustered around a woman. Usually, it was he who initiated the lewd innuendos. But Portia wasn't your average woman.

"What I'd like to do to you," she purred as she tousled his hair.

Portia straightened up and walked back toward the middle of the room. "Look, you guys figure it out. The way I see it, we don't have much time. The phase is almost over." She fixed herself another shot of tequila and sat herself down on the wing chair opposite me. "Tick, tock," she toasted before tossing back the Mexican Gold.

Just as quickly as she appeared, she was gone. Natalie stirred in the chair. "Damn, I can already feel tomorrow's hangover. How much did she drink?"

"Only three shots, but you gave her a head start. I think you're just drained from her taking over," I said.

"Did she give anything up?"

"No, but I think she wanted to give it up to Ty," I laughed. Okay, it wasn't funny, and it certainly wasn't the time to joke, but it was pretty comical seeing him sitting there all uncomfortable.

Tyler finally broke out of his daze. "Dude! That bitch is a trip. Do you think she's really into me?"

Twenty-Nine

I woke up with a profound hangover—but it wasn't for the good cause I'd hoped. We learned absolutely nothing from talking with Portia. Sure, our plan to speak with her worked, but we got nothing for all our efforts. Knowing that alone stung more than the piercing pain in my head.

My body refused to move, so I continued to lay in bed, replaying the events of the previous night. As far as we knew, Portia had yet to commit any physical harm against anyone, but that didn't stop me from fearing her. We had always assumed that at some point she would take control over Natalie's body and that would be the end of it. But to hear Portia tell it, both souls would perish as Natalie's body continued to deteriorate if we didn't do something about it and fast. That more than anything else scared the shit out of me.

The clock on my nightstand told me I wasn't too late for breakfast. If I was going to come up with another plan, I'd have to refuel, not to mention get rid of this te-kill-ya hangover. I forced myself out of bed, knowing what would happen if I didn't come down for breakfast.

As I struggled to leave the bedroom, I ran into my mother—who not surprisingly, was in the same shape I was. I wondered what her excuse was. Vodka? Gin? We passed each other without saying a word as I went down the staircase and she in the opposite direction toward the bathroom.

I found Carmen hovering over the stove. I slid into the closest chair and stretched my arms over the kitchen table for balance. I wondered how the smell of bacon grease could be both enticing and revolting at the same time. It took every ounce of strength to get out of bed to come down for breakfast; I wasn't so sure I had it in me to actually eat breakfast.

The sizzling sound of the thinly sliced pork kept perfect rhythm with the sound of Carmen clicking her tongue. *Click, click.* She didn't have to say anything. I knew she disapproved of my staying out all night drinking, especially since she knew how sensitive I was to my own mother's condition. When I was a teen, she always knew when I snuck out of the house or broke curfew. She always knew the comings and goings of this house better than anyone—like an omnipotent force—I always suspected she had a third eye.

"Don't even say it, Carmen. I feel bad enough already."

She turned around and pointed the fork she was holding at me. "*No creas que no sé*," she scolded. God bless her for keeping her voice just above a whisper. Anything louder and I was liable to get nauseated again, which would give a whole new meaning to the breakfast otherwise known as *huevos revueltos*.

"Know what?" She couldn't possibly know what we were up to last night. I'm still not entirely sure I knew what we were doing last night. It was all a blur to me at that point, but I knew with certainty that whatever it was, it was unsuccessful. Portia wasn't forthcoming about anything of value, and I had the distinct impression it was because she didn't know herself.

But I wasn't getting anything more out of Carmen of what she knew or didn't. But it didn't matter, she'd already turned her back to me to focus on the bacon. For all I knew she was only talking about me being drunk. Then again, it was Carmen, and she always seemed to know all.

☾

I met up with Tyler and Natalie at Hector's—hoping a little hair of the dog would cure what ailed me—and for once, I was the last to arrive. It was slowly starting to become one of our daily haunts, as we couldn't speak as freely at the The Pit with the sisters always there. Watching them from the door, I wondered what it would be like to have met Natalie under more normal circumstances—to be able to walk into a bar to see my best friend and my best girl waiting for me without a care in the world. No magic, no drama, just a couple of twenty-somethings getting together for a drink.

"How's everyone feeling today?" I asked, making my way over to the bar. I did my best to sound positive in spite of our failed attempt to get anywhere with Portia the night before. The outcome was indeed a failure, but we tried, which was more than I could say for anyone else involved.

"Well, I lucked out. No hangover," Natalie said. She may have sounded okay, but I could tell she was miserable —hangover or not.

Tyler took a sip of his Bloody Mary before answering. "I wish I could say the same."

Hector noted my arrival and moved over to the side of the bar where I joined my friends. If we were here at this morning hour, he knew a beer wouldn't quite cut it this time. "What'll it be?"

I looked down over at Tyler's Bloody Mary and Natalie's beer. "Make it a michelada," I said, thinking I'd have the best of both worlds. I hadn't had one since I moved to Louisiana and at the moment, it was just what the doctor ordered. The ingredients were simple enough that I could enjoy them back home in New Orleans, but it was much more satisfying when someone else made it for you.

Hector must have sensed my pounding headache, so he whipped up the beer and clamato concoction in a flash, adding spices and Worcheshire sauce in the process. The best part was the salt and lime mixture on the rim of the glass. And around these parts, a good michelada could cure just about anything.

"Last night was a bust," Natalie said. "We're still no closer to figuring out how to deal with Portia. Do we have any other bright ideas?"

Before, she had scoffed all my attempts to help rid her sister's soul, resigned to the fact that it was her fate to keep her sister trapped inside her body. But now, she appeared desperate after having heard what Portia had to say about the subject. I don't think she ever really considered the possibility that they could both die. She didn't have to say it, but I also knew that despite her sister's actions, she still loved her.

"I'm all tapped out," I said. "Ty?"

He was barely following along in the conversation, focusing on his Bloody Mary instead. He must have had more tequila than I realized. "Huh? Oh, no. This is all you guys. I'm just along for the ride," he said.

"We've gone over everything she said last night and none of it was useful. I'm afraid we're out of options," Natalie said.

"Wait, not so fast. She did say something that caught my attention, but I'm still trying to figure it out what it means," I said.

Natalie looked hopeful for a second. "What was it?"

"Something about the phase being almost over. What do you think she meant by that?"

"I have no clue," she said.

"Great. Now we're back to square one."

"Look guys, I'm all up for another grand adventure, but next time, let's not involve booze, okay? At least for a few days," Tyler said.

We all agreed to call it a day from brainstorming. With Portia running around and the uncertainty of their lives, we weren't sure how much time we really had.

After paying the tab, Natalie went to the restaurant to spend time with her aunts at the restaurant, while Tyler decided he would go back to sleep. Not really having anywhere to go myself, I went home, hoping this would be the day my mother was coherent enough to visit with.

Thirty

My mother was nowhere to be found when I got back to the house. She was probably already in bed nursing her own hangover. I really wasn't expecting to have a heart to heart moment with her, but I'd be a hypocrite if I didn't have some hope for a reconciliation between us. If I were to have faith in Natalie, I should also hold out hope for me and my mother.

Carmen was absent for most of the day—it was Sunday, her day off—so I took the opportunity to do more research on the Great Priests and the book. While I only skimmed through the finer points before, this time I spent more time searching for hidden meanings and messages in the text. After several hours of reading, I was still no closer to finding out the answers than before I swiped the book.

I'd laid in bed for a good portion of the morning, enjoying a moment of solitude. When I set out to come home for the summer, I had expected to reach out to old friends and relax before I began med school. Never in my wildest dreams did I ever expect to be involved with an honest to God healer—or nightmares, if you included Portia. So I slept.

When I finally woke, my stomach got the better of me, so I headed downstairs to fix myself a late breakfast. I hadn't checked my watch, so it could have been well past lunch. Regardless, there was a box of Cap'n Crunch with my name written all over it. Carmen always had a box in the pantry for me.

At some point, as I was slurping the remaining milk from the bowl, my mother had wandered into the hallway that separated the kitchen from the living room. For a second there, I actually thought she was going to come in and join me, but she just paced up and down the hall with no destination. After watching her for a few moments, I realized she was singing.

"When one is two and the moon is full."
"When two is one and the moon is new."

It reminded me of what Big Momma Ledoux had said back in New Orleans: *Two souls. They struggle. Only one will triumph.* But what did that mean? Was my mother talking about Natalie? I didn't know how it was all connected, if there was even a connection at all, but I didn't believe in coincidences.

"When one is two and the moon is full," she kept chanting, louder this time, as if she were taunting me. "When two is one and the moon is new."

I got up from the table and went into the hall after her. "Stop talking in riddles!" I yelled at her, regretting it instantly as quickly as it came out of my mouth. My little outburst sent my mother running up the stairs and slamming her bedroom door. My frustration was evident as I paced around the hallway, doing exactly what she had been doing only moments before. A guy can only take so much, and I was finally beginning to crack under pressure.

"You no understand, Wyatt," Carmen said, placing her hand on my arm. I didn't even know she had returned home. She seemed to have appeared out of nowhere. But that was Carmen's style; always around when you needed her, when you least expected.

"What? That my mother is a drunk and no longer has the ability to form a coherent thought?"

"*Mijito*, you know she more than that."

"Know what? That she's crazy too?"

"Wyatt!"

I had taken it too far, as far as Carmen was concerned, but it was true and she knew it. I was tired of her excusing my mom for being a poor mother. Carmen was the one who raised me for Christ's sake! She had been a constant figure my whole life and most of my mother's. She knew better than anyone the downward spiral my mother had taken, so why did she insist on defending her?

"You no understand," she said again in her broken Spanish. "Your mother teach me."

"Teach you what?" It was hard for me to imagine my mother teaching anyone anything. I'd missed out on the simple things a mother teaches her son, like how to ride a bike, how to talk to girls—it was all left to Carmen. Hell, she even taught me how to shave when I was old enough to hold a razor.

"The cards. *La magia.*"

Magic? "What are you saying?" I asked, more to myself than for Carmen's benefit.

Carmen nodded, tears falling down the side of her face. "She a powerful *bruja* once."

A slow piercing pain spread throughout my body leaving me numb. "She's like Natalie isn't she?" I had to sit down, but we were still standing in the hallway. I braced myself against the wall for support.

"*Sí.*" She came close and tried to hug me, but I slid away from her.

"You're right, I don't understand. Start talking, Carmen."

"When your mother little, I came to work here. I knew *brujería* from village, so I came to help your mother grown into a powerful *bruja*."

"Wait, I'm confused. I thought *brujas* only practiced black magic? Are you saying my mother is a dark witch?"

"No, *mijito*, *brujas* are both good and bad. Her family brought me to help your mother grow into powers. She very beautiful, your mother, and I was not only one to help her." Another tear rolled down her cheek.

"The De Leóns." It had to be the sisters. Who else could it be other than them? They were the only ones knowledgeable enough about magic to help guide my mother, much like they were guiding Natalie. And right about now, I was just as mad at them as I was at Carmen from keeping this a secret from me.

Carmen was about to say something, but stopped short as if she'd changed her mind, and then simply nodded in confirmation.

With everything that happened in my mother's life, no wonder she went off the deep end. Why hadn't anyone ever told me about any of this? It's not like I was completely ignorant on the subject. I grew up with Carmen casting spells and for years witnessed people come to our property to get their readings done. Did it not occur to anyone that it might be important, even useful maybe, that I know of my mother's past? Perhaps I wouldn't have listened or even believed it, but I would have been more empathetic toward my mother. Maybe if I knew, I never would have left Caldero.

I calmed down enough to listen to what Carmen was telling me. It was too late to repair the past, but I could still try to understand to forge a decent future between us. "Does that mean you're a Healer, too?"

"No, *mijito*. I am very strong, yes, but not like your *madre*."

I understood what she was saying. She was a *curandera*, with limited powers no doubt, but nothing more. My mother was an only child. Carmen was like the sister she never had—someone to guard and protect her. To be her companion. I got that now. It wasn't Carmen who had healed my swollen wrist all those years ago, it was my mother. Whenever I suffered an injury as a child, my mother was always around to kiss it and "make it better." To a child, there was nothing unusual about that. Only in her case, it was in the literal sense.

Understanding things a little better now, I went straight for the kitchen, banging cupboards and pulling out everything that was in the way of the task at hand. I had a plan. I was going to hear all this from my mother herself.

"*Siéntate*. I make you something," Carmen said, confused by my erratic actions in her kitchen.

"No, I'm not sitting down and I'm not hungry. I'm making strong-ass coffee to wake her up. I'm going to get answers from her tonight, even if it means pouring it down her throat with a funnel until she sobers up." I wasn't being overly sympathetic, but desperate times called for desperate measures. My gut was telling me my mother knew many of the answers I sought.

"*Siéntate*," Carmen ordered once again. "Coffee not enough. I wake her up." She pushed me toward the kitchen table for me to sit while she began to pull what random ingredients from the pantry, while cleaning up the mess I'd made.

"What are you making? Some kind of witch's hangover brew?" I wasn't being disingenuous, I was genuinely curious.

Carmen only hummed in response. Watching her in the kitchen was like watching an artist at work. She was wrong about being a true witch. Her graceful moves around the room, coupled with the meticulous precision in measuring the ingredients was pure magic.

So as not to upset my mother any more than she already was, I allowed Carmen to approach her. I waited in the living room, hoping that after a few minutes, my mother would come back down and join us.

Five minutes turned into ten and Carmen returned downstairs alone. I had been so hopeful, but I can't say I was surprised.

"She need rest. Tomorrow," she promised.

What was it my mother had said all those years ago before leaving for Tulane? *Promises and obligations… Only they weren't promises. Not to me.*

In the next few days, my mother never did sober up long enough to have that talk with me. Not even at Carmen's urging. I guess she couldn't deal with that either.

☾

I couldn't get my mother's rhyme from the other day out of my head. When one is two and the moon is full. When two is one and the moon is new.

The phase is almost over, Portia had said.

It was a simple as a nursery rhyme.

The night we got plastered and spoke to Portia, there was a full moon out. I was well aware there were other phases in between, but the next significant phase was the new moon. She was talking about a lunar phase! I scrambled to my laptop and looked up the date of the next new moon.

Once I had everything figured out—the meaning of my mother's riddle, Big Momma's palm reading, and Portia's warning—Natalie and I began to formulate another plan, but in order for it to work, we had to involve Carmen and her aunts. An ambush was our best bet to ensure their cooperation. The only problem was, we couldn't figure out a way to get them all together without them being suspicious.

Natalie had the idea to invite Carmen and I over for dinner, but we would soon be given the best possible excuse to have everyone under one roof.

In three weeks, we'd have our window of opportunity.

Thirty-One

A tropical depression hit the night of the next new moon. It was a miracle of sorts.

Those of us who grew up in the Gulf were always on alert during hurricane season. Up until a day or two before any big storm got closer to land, no one knew exactly which path it would take. By morning, the weather service confirmed the storm's trajectory was headed right in our direction.

Preparations were made all over town before the storm was scheduled to hit, our own house being no exception. Carmen was glad I was home so I could install plywood over the windows. A tropical depression wasn't as major as a hurricane, but it could be destructive nonetheless. After I finished taping the windows inside with a large X, preventing shards of glass from flying if struck by strong winds, I headed over to the De León's to storm-proof their house.

They sky was getting darker, a sign of the impending storm approaching, as I drove my pick-up over to the De León's and I wondered whether or not they should vacate their home. It had been years since their house had seen any type of structural renovations. Even a leak on the roof was cause for concern. I wasn't sure if they would be safe.

As I drove up the drive, I saw Amelia hammering planks of four-by-fours against the window frames and I realized that the old women were ill equipped to secure the house during an emergency—what they needed were solid sheets of plywood.

"*Izquierda, tonta*!" Ester yelled up at her sister.

This wasn't good. Things must be bad if they were already fighting over the placement of the boards.

"Don't call me stupid. I know what I'm doin'," Amelia yelled back from the ladder on which she was perched. Ester was trying to lead her sister further left of the window pane without much success. She was dangerously close to driving a nail through the glass.

"You're going to hit the *vidrio*. *Izquierda*!"

Having had enough of name calling, Amelia climbed down the ladder, no doubt saving herself and the house from possible injury.

I immediately grabbed the hammer from Amelia. "Stop. I'll go back home and bring over some of the extra plywood we had left over. The boards you have aren't going to do."

"*Te lo dije*," Ester said, looking smug.

"Oh, thank goodness you're here, Wyatt! Ester and I were going crazy not knowing what to do. Luis usually handles all this for us, but he went to Refugio yesterday to visit his sick sister before the storm arrived," she said. Luis was one of the part-time servers at the restaurant and I always suspected he also doubled as a handy man whenever the sisters needed help around the house.

"I'm always happy to lend a hand. Hey, on second thought, why don't all y'all come over to our house. There's plenty of room for everyone. I can take you over now, then come back on my own to board up your house."

"Is there enough time? They're predicting the storm to hit soon," she said.

"There's plenty of time," I assured her.

"I'll have to see what Ester and Natalie think, but I think it's a good idea, thank you."

Ester and Natalie had no reservations about coming over to my house to wait out the storm. We had plenty of provisions, thanks to Carmen, and the house was big enough for six people to be comfortable enough without getting in each other's way. But for what Natalie and I had in mind, it was a moot point.

With the storm proofing taken care of and everyone safe and out of harm's way at Casa McKenna, Natalie and I made our announcement. As soon as we sat them down to explain what we wanted to do, not everyone was thrilled with the plan. But in the end, we finally convinced her aunts and Carmen that we ought to at least try to perform another ritual to cast out Portia's soul. With Portia coming out more regularly, it posed a great risk not only to Natalie, but to everyone else involved. The women were reluctant at first, not wanting to go against the church and their warnings, but they finally relented after we told them about Tequila Night and all that Portia had said.

If my mother's rhyme was correct—since she couldn't handle being bothered to speak to me, and that was a big if—considering she was drunk when she said it, Portia's soul would revert back to one when the moon was new. We didn't know if it would work, but it was our best chance to save Natalie.

Carmen and the sisters decided the best place to hold the cleansing ritual was in the old barn out back. Since they did not know the strength of Portia's true power, they thought it wise to keep the damage to a minimum—heaven forbid my mother's living room got trashed in the process.

I didn't know if holding a casting in the barn during a major storm was a bright idea, but the women insisted. The barn behind our house was stable enough, but whether or not it was secure enough to keep us safe in this kind of storm was anyone's guess. We were taking a lot of chances with our lives that night. Fortunately for us, it was a short walk from the main house.

The winds howled as the women settled themselves in the middle of the earthen floor. For now, the place remained free of water. I only hoped the old structure held out. The barn had remained unscathed through countless storms and hurricanes, but it would be just our luck if it decided to give out tonight. With nothing to contribute to the ritual, I moved toward the back of the barn, anxious to see if the prophecy of the new moon would finally free Natalie of her sister.

Out of the corner of my eye, I noticed a sudden movement hidden deep in the shadows. We were using lanterns to illuminate the barn, and the light didn't carry far, but I could make out a heavyset image. With everything happening so fast, I didn't have time to wonder what the hell it was. I only cared about Natalie. But right at that moment, the figure stepped out from the shadows and revealed herself.

It was Big Momma Ledoux, the old voodoo woman from New Orleans.

"It be good to see you again, *cher*," she said.

"What the hell are you doing here?"

"Ah, *cher*, I told you. Your destiny be here."

How in the world did she get here during the raging storm? For that matter, how in the world did she know we would be here in the first place? She had to have been hidden in the barn before we got here. How was that possible? "I hope you're here to help."

Amelia answered for the old voodoo woman. "She is. I'm the one that called her."

"I don't understand."

"You think we don't know what goes on between the two of you?" she said, meaning me and Natalie. "We knew you two had some kind of plan brewing for tonight, so we called Big Momma in anticipation."

"During a tropical depression?"

Big Momma Ledoux winked. "There ain't no storm that can keep Big Momma away," she said. "My nephew Johnny drives a rig. Brought me down last night before the nasty come."

I still didn't understand. What was Big Momma doing here?

"You've been away a long time, Wyatt. Ester and I had to find a way to bring you back home in order to help our Natalie. It was no accident that you went to Big Momma's shop. Nor was it a conscious decision on your part when you suddenly decided to come home. She made that possible," Amelia said.

The aging voodoo priestess nodded, confirming everything Amelia just said. "It took a lot of juju to push you home, boy."

"But why? Why was it so important that I come here and help Natalie?"

"Because Natalie needed something to fight for," Amelia said. "Love."

We had never spoken about love. There was no doubt I loved Natalie, but we had never said the words to each other. I went over to where Natalie was standing. "Is this true?"

"For awhile I just gave up. Then you had to come along," she said with a smile. "I love you and I'm willing to do whatever it takes."

That's all I needed to hear. "I love you, too." And in front of all the other women in the room, I kissed her.

The Wheel of Fortune card. The reading Natalie gave me that first time over breakfast. She said it meant that forces beyond my control had a hand in changing my fate. From the beginning, I suspected Big Momma had something to do with my return to Caldero, but the reality of it didn't sink in until now. Magical forces were real and I'd been a fool to think otherwise. There were forces of nature at play that were beyond my comprehension. I looked at the voodoo woman and back at Amelia. "So, you really do know Big Momma?"

"*Por supuesto.* Who do you think gave us the gumbo recipe?" Ester chimed in.

Now that everyone had settled into their positions, the women made a blessing to the saints and began to recite some ritual chant as Natalie laid down on the ground. After all these years, I figured Carmen was an amateur healer, one that couldn't compare to the status of the two sisters that sat next to her. Now, I realize that she is much stronger than I ever gave her credit for.

Meanwhile, Big Momma Ledoux circled around the trio, sprinkling what looked like ground-up chalk around the women and chanting something I couldn't understand. Whatever it was, I hoped it worked.

As for Carmen and the sisters, I couldn't make out the words they themselves were chanting, they were going so fast, but I knew whatever it was they were chanting was mixed with some of the prayers I'd learned as a kid I'd long forgotten until now. Heavenly prayers mixed with whatever else Big Momma was chanting.

Natalie's body began to move, seizing and convulsing at every other word all four women chanted. And for every other word uttered, her back would arch, as if there were demons inside yearning to come out. Watching her go through this was agony and despite their warnings, I wanted to grab Natalie up into my arms and relieve her of the pain she was most likely experiencing.

"It's not working," I yelled out in frustration. I felt helpless, not being able to help the women or Natalie. And my attempts to appeal to the four women went unnoticed as they continued to recite the ritualistic prayers.

"Natalie, can you hear me? It's going to be okay, I promise." I had no idea whether this would work or not, or if she could even hear me, but it was all I could offer her at the moment.

The storm continued to grumble something fierce on the outside, as the violent storm between the two souls commenced in the inside. The door to the barn struggled to open against the harsh winds, and a figure burst through. It was Father Hilario, and he wasn't alone.

"I thought I could be of some assistance," he said. "And I brought reinforcements."

In the flowing nightgown I began to think of as her uniform, my mother emerged from behind him. "Wyatt," she said softly, with enough meaning behind it to apologize for everything. "I can help."

I had to do a double take at what I was seeing. For the first time in years, my mother appeared sober and lucid. Granted, she looked frail, like she had been the victim of a coma, only having just awoken from a deep sleep that left her movements mechanical and slow, but she was here. She was drenched from the rain outside, her nightgown sheer from the moisture, but aside from that, I hadn't seen her look so good in years. Whatever Father

Hilario did to make her come out of her stupor, I was forever grateful.

Before I could barrage my mother with questions, Amelia called out to her. "Catherine, quick, take hold of my hand."

I watched as my mother took part of the circle that was to save Natalie's life. Father Hilario also walked toward chanting women and began to recite a prayer of his own from a little black prayer book. In his other hand, he grasped a small clear jar, which I assumed was filled with holy water. I didn't understand half of what was going on with so many people involved, but I was thankful for their intervention. If it could save Natalie, I was open to anything.

"The gris-gris I gave you. Put it in her hand," Big Momma ordered.

I was glad I had taken her advice and kept the pouch with me at all times and I did what was asked of me, grateful to be of assistance. The five women broke the circle in order for me to get close to Natalie. I took the small pouch from my pocket and placed it in Natalie's hand, closing her fingers around it.

The women quickly reverted back to their positions around Natalie's body and clasped hands.

Seconds went by. "It's not working," I cried again, but no one seemed to be paying any attention to me.

I could hear the winds die down outside. And in an instant everything went quiet. Not just the storm, but in the old barn. Natalie had stopped struggling and the chanting ceased. Her body lay limp on the ground. Did it work? I looked to Father Hilario for confirmation. His eyes were fixated on the glass jar he still held in his hand.

"What's that for anyway?" I finally had the chance to ask.

"I brought it to contain Portia's soul upon being expelled from Natalie's body," he said

Only, it was empty.

Or was I not capable of seeing a soul? I didn't know if that was good or bad. Did souls even appear in colors? White for good, black for bad? Would we even know if the soul had been captured? For some reason I imagined the jar would resemble a lava lamp with a colored floating mass after the Portia's soul was transferred. For all I knew, the human soul was transparent, invisible to the naked eye. Again, I looked to the priest for some sort of sign that the ritual was a success.

"I'm sorry," was all he would say.

I dropped to my knees next Natalie's body and cried. I went to hug her lifeless body on the floor when I felt the faint beating of her heart. For the briefest of moments, I thought she was dead. "She's still with us!"

The women remained silent as the priest came to check on Natalie. "She's alive," he confirmed. "Her breath is very shallow, but Wyatt's right, she is still with us."

"What does that mean?" I asked. "Did Portia's soul leave her body or what?"

Natalie's eyelids fluttered as her eyes adjusted to the dim light in the room. "What happened?"

"We don't know," I said. "How do you feel?"

"Different. I feel different somehow."

That couldn't be a good sign, but I kept that to myself. "It'll be okay whatever it is," I said instead, as I held her in my arms.

Big Momma Ledoux came closer to us. She took Natalie's hand and gently pulled it toward her, palm up. "The soul lines are one. One soul has triumphed."

I didn't understand what she was saying. "Tell us what that means," I said. I was done playing nice.

"They are now one."

A single tear trickled down Natalie's cheek. She seemed to understand what the old voodoo woman was saying.

"Natalie?" I asked. "Are you okay? What does that mean?" Either they were successful in expelling Portia, or Natalie absorbed her sister permanently, joining both souls into one.

"Honey." It was my mother speaking to me now, trying to lift me up from the ground where Natalie lay. "Perhaps Natalie needs some time to digest this."

"Digest what? Will someone explain to me what the hell is going on?"

My mother pulled on my arm to get me to stand. "Wyatt, please. Give her time."

I'd never seen my mother act so maternal as she did at that moment. Momentarily stunned, I got up and obeyed.

"Just tell me, please. Is she going to be okay?" I looked over at Natalie, the woman I loved, as I asked this, searching for answers to the questions no one was willing to part with.

"Wyatt, come. I will explain everything back at the house," the priest said.

Reluctantly, I left Natalie still sitting on the floor, being consoled by her aunts.

But there was one last question I had to ask before I left the women. There was one thing I had to know. "What was in that pouch?" I asked Big Momma.

"Faith," she crooned, her pearly white teeth visible, glowing in the semi-darkness.

"That's it? Just faith? Nothing magical?"

"Oh, *cher*. Tis magic. Tis magic because you believe."

Thirty-Two

The storm had died down to a heavy rain as I followed Father Hidalgo into the house. He helped himself to a Scotch once we settled into the living room. I was actually surprised my mother had left any liquor in the house for the priest to find.

I sat across from him and waited for him to say something about what happened back at the barn. The priest just sat there, swirling the gold liquid in the glass tumbler, with a vacant expression on his face. It was almost as if he had seen a ghost.

After staring at him for a few minutes, I got tired of waiting for him to say something. "What happens next? Do we know if Portia's really gone?"

The old priest, with the aging white hair, shook his head solemnly. "I do not have the answers. I wish I could offer you some words of wisdom or comfort, but I cannot."

"Some Great Priest you turned out to be," I mumbled under my breath. The ritual seemed successful, yet we were sitting here still searching for answers.

"Do not be angry my son," he said. "And I am not a Great Priest."

I was momentarily stunned by his admission. I had assumed, ever since that day I went to see him at St. Cecilia's, that he was. He never gave me any reason not to. "But Natalie said—"

The old priest continued, "The one assigned to this parish abandoned us long ago, leaving me with his secrets but nothing more. I am sorry I gave you the impression I could offer you more."

Now I understood the glazed-over look in his eyes. I don't think the priest really believed in any of this. Since he wasn't a Great Priest, he couldn't fully understand or appreciate the severity of the situation. I imagine it was like the small bible he clutched during the ritual out in the barn. People believe and swear oaths to the great book. They take every word and miracle documented in it as truth. But if one was lucky enough to actually see a miracle take place, they'd come to the realization that they didn't truly believe at all, until that actual moment when they witnessed it firsthand.

"Hold on," I ran upstairs to my bedroom before the priest could say anything more and came back down carrying the book I had stolen from him.

"Here," I said. "I'm sorry I took it from the church." I had initially thought he was a Great Priest who wasn't doing anything in order to save Natalie when in reality, he was just an old priest shouldering someone else's burden.

He simply nodded in acknowledgment as he took the book from my grasp. "I knew you would take it the moment I showed it to you."

"Sorry," I said again.

"It's alright my son. Thank you for returning it."

Something he said earlier didn't sit well with me. "None of this makes any sense you know. If Natalie was sent here to be protected by her aunts, surely they would have assigned a new Great Priest here to replace the one that left." Not that I believed for one second they would offer anything useful, but if their organization claimed to be the ones to guard and protect the Healers, why did leave Natalie to fight this battle on her own?

"I cannot answer that. All I can tell you is that I have involved myself more than I have been allowed to. I will continue to offer my assistance, but I am afraid my help is limited."

"So the last Great Priest just jumped ship and abandoned everyone? Why?"

Father Hidalgo nodded. "It was best for the Guardians of the Watch that he resign his post immediately. He stayed on for a long while, but then he couldn't live under the trappings of a normal life. He left both this town and this parish indefinitely."

"Why? What did he do that he had to go and couldn't be replaced?"

"There are some things I am willing to share with you, but this is a matter that I am bound by confidentiality. I am sure you understand." From the tone in his voice, I could tell he knew I didn't understand and without having to say the words, I also knew he was sorry he couldn't elaborate more. In a way, I respected him for that. But that didn't mean I had to like it.

"No, I don't, but I guess I don't really have a choice now do I? So what now, *Padre*? Is it truly over? Is Natalie free from the curse you people placed on her?"

"I believe Portia is gone, yes. But as to the ramifications of what just transpired, I cannot venture to guess. You two, especially Natalia, will have to be careful."

"So it's not over."

"No, I do not believe it is."

"And my mother? How did you manage to get through to her?"

"Catherine only needed to be reminded of what an extraordinary woman she is," he said. "And we prayed."

Perhaps I needed to reconsider my position regarding the power of prayer. "Thank you for that."

☾

It'd been almost a week since the casting and I'd barely seen Natalie. Either she hadn't been hanging around The Pit or she refused to see me at her house. I didn't fight it, as I knew she'd been through a lot and I wanted to give her as much space as she needed. The few times I did manage to set my eyes on her around town, however, I noticed she was thinner than usual, with dark circles under her eyes.

By the seventh day, I'd had all I could take of her freeze out and went over to see her whether she wanted me to or not. This time, I was prepared for a fight. Only, instead of making excuses for not seeing me, she let me through the door. Perhaps she'd finally made peace with what happened and was ready to put it behind her.

That was when I noticed the luggage lined up near the bottom of the staircase. "What's all this?"

"I have to go find her, Wyatt."

"Who? Portia? What are you talking about?"

"I don't expect you to understand, but when they first pulled her soul, I was relieved to have her gone. But now, I feel like a part of me is missing. I have to find her, Wyatt."

This was not the conversation I was expecting when I came over to the house. I imagined we would be discussing our future together. But not this. "You don't even know if she's still alive! For all we know, her soul died when they took it out of you." Father Hidalgo couldn't give me a definite answer, but I took his advice to heart. We both had to be careful, not knowing what transpired on Portia's side of the equation.

"That's the point. We don't know. I have to find out for myself where they kept her body to see if she's really gone. I won't be able to rest until I know for sure."

"Do you even know where they kept her?" The Great Priests had guarded the location of Portia's physical body and it was doubtful even Father Hidalgo knew where to find her. He said it himself, he was not a Great Priest. Somehow I found it highly doubtful he would be privy to such information.

"I know, but I won't stop until I do."

"Assuming she's dead," I point out. But if her sister somehow managed to survive, Natalie would be putting herself in danger. There was no way I was going to let her go traipsing around looking for someone who could ultimately kill her if she got in the way.

"No. Assuming she's alive. I don't think she's gone. Call it sisterly intuition, but I believe she's still out there."

"And what if she is? Do you think she'll be sticking around? She could be anywhere!"

"Then I'll *go* anywhere."

"So this is it. You're just going to pack up your bags and leave." Incredible. We spent the summer trying to rid her of Portia.

"Yes. It's what I have to do. I need to see her for myself."

"Then let me go with you." I would defer medical school for a year if it meant I could be with her.

"I can't let you do that. You have a great opportunity in front of you. To help others. I should know, I have the power to heal. Besides, I have to do this alone. If she's still alive, I don't know what she's capable of doing to you. You've witnessed it firsthand, she's a powerful witch and I can't risk losing you."

"You'll lose me anyway if you don't let me come with you." I didn't mean for it to come out as an ultimatum, but it was still the truth. Didn't she see that? If she'd only let me go with her, we could be together. She didn't have to face this alone.

"You'd be safe back in New Orleans. I'm sorry, Wyatt."

"So that's it then, end of discussion, you're going to just pick up and leave."

"That about sums it up," she said. "I wish you'd support my decision."

"I wish I did, too."

There was nothing more I could say at that point. She'd made up her mind and this was one battle I wouldn't be able to win. I didn't want to say goodbye. I didn't want to leave Caldero. I didn't want to lose Natalie.

"Well, I guess this is goodbye then," I said, not wanting to let her see how hurt I actually was. "If you ever come back, or find yourself in New Orleans, look me up."

She flashed me a brilliant smile. "Oh, I imagine I'll be seeing you around, cowboy."

Epilogue

Somewhere, on an Indian reservation in Arizona…

Chanting could be heard from outside the empty tomb where The Evil One once laid.

To be continued....

Acknowledgments

This story could not have been written without all of the stories and colorful characters I grew up with living in the Rio Grande Valley. While fictional, Caldero, TX is a mash-up of all the places, persons, restaurants, cities, and events I enjoyed while living in the Lone Star State. I didn't know it then, but looking back, I realize I had the time of my life growing up in South Texas. So, thank you.

Thank you dear husband, Dave Lefeve (resident chef consultant), for your lesson on the differences between Creole and Cajun gumbo, among other things.

I also could not have written this without the guidance and support of all my beta readers: Charisse Berree, Kristy Feltenberger Gillespie, Sandra Pedraza, Laura Ybarra, and my mom, Irene Ybarra, who proofed all my Spanish for accuracy. And a big thank you goes out to Shauna Granger, who read my book, told me what she really thought, and made me make it better.

And I'd be remiss if I did not include a special thank you to Jeff Bryan (aka J.L. Bryan), who always accepts my manuscripts for editing just under the wire.

About the Author

Claudia Lefeve was born and raised in the Gulf Coast border town of Brownsville, Texas; a curious place where folks see curanderas in lieu of shrinks, tortillas are served at every meal, and even gringos speak Spanish. She currently resides in Northern Virginia with her husband, one precocious pug, and a rambunctious chocolate lab.

www.claudialefeve.com
www.facebook.com/claudialefeve
@claudialefeve

Extras

Check out my Darkly Beings board on Pinterest (under Claudia Lefeve) for photos of places, foods, and all things inspired...

If you'd like to read more about Kiki and Chris and what happened that fateful night in Eagle Pass, the short story "*Kiki and The Lone Stranger*" will be published in the anthology, *Coffin Hop: Death by Drive-In,* featuring works from some of the best indie horror writers around. Available this fall, proceeds from this anthology will benefit a charitable literacy organization.

The tarot cards used by Natalie in *Darkly Beings* is called the *Vanessa Tarot*, created by Lynyrd Narciso, taking inspiration from pop culture: television, cinema, comics, and real life heroines (there really is a card that looks like Vanna White).